THE DARK KNIGHT™

THE DARK KNIGHT™

Junior Novelization

by Stacia Deutsch and Rhody Cohon

Adapted from the film *The Dark Knight*

Screenplay by Jonathan Nolan and Christopher Nolan

Story by Christopher Nolan & David S. Goyer

Batman created by Bob Kane

A FILM BY CHRISTOPHER NOLAN

WARNER BROS. PICTURES PRESENTS

IN ASSOCIATION WITH LEGENDARY PICTURES A SYNCOPY PRODUCTION A FILM BY CHRISTOPHER NOLAN CHRISTIAN BALE "THE DARK KNIGHT" MICHAEL CAINE HEATH LEDGER GARY OLDMAN AARON ECKHART MAGGIE GYLLENHAAL AND MORGAN FREEMAN MUSIC BY HANS ZIMMER JAMES NEWTON HOWARD COSTUME DESIGNER LINDY HEMMING EDITOR LEE SMITH, A.C.E. PRODUCTION DESIGNER NATHAN CROWLEY DIRECTOR OF PHOTOGRAPHY WALLY PFISTER, A.S.C. EXECUTIVE PRODUCERS BENJAMIN MELNIKER MICHAEL E. USLAN KEVIN DE LA NOY THOMAS TULL BASED UPON BATMAN CHARACTERS CREATED BY BOB KANE AND PUBLISHED BY DC COMICS STORY BY CHRISTOPHER NOLAN & DAVID S. GOYER SCREENPLAY BY JONATHAN NOLAN AND CHRISTOPHER NOLAN PRODUCED BY CHARLES ROVEN EMMA THOMAS CHRISTOPHER NOLAN DIRECTED BY CHRISTOPHER NOLAN

 LEGENDARY PICTURES   SYNCOPY PG-13 PARENTS STRONGLY CAUTIONED Some Material May Be Inappropriate for Children Under 13. INTENSE SEQUENCES OF VIOLENCE AND SOME MENACE Soundtrack Album on Warner Sunset/Warner Bros. Records TM & © DC Comics WARNER BROS. PICTURES ©2008 Warner Bros. Ent. All Rights Reserved

WWW.THEDARKKNIGHT.COM

   HarperCollins *Children's Books*

First published in the UK by HarperCollins Children's Books in 2008

1 3 5 7 9 10 8 6 4 2

ISBN-10: x

ISBN-13: 978-0-00-727725-4

Printed and bound in Great Britain

THE DARK KNIGHT™

Chapter One

In a shadowed alley of Gotham City, a man was about to buy drugs from a dealer. The dealer reached into his jacket pocket to pull out a small, sealed plastic bag when suddenly something in the sky caught his eye. It was a beam of light. A glowing shaft illuminating the otherwise dark and starless night.

The light stretched from the top of Gotham's Major Crimes Unit, the MCU, straight up, casting the image of a bat over all of Gotham City.

The Bat-Signal.

The dealer's hand twitched. He couldn't sell his wares tonight. The glowing sign of the bat made him too nervous. "No way, man," he said, tucking his stash back into his pocket and turning away from the man with the cash. "I don't like it tonight."

The buyer waved bills in his face, showing the dealer how much money he was going to lose if he walked away. "What're you, superstitious?" he taunted. "You got more chance of winning the lottery than running into *him*…"

It didn't matter. The trade was over. Without even appearing at the scene, Batman, the lone vigilante stalking the night and protecting Gotham's citizens, had prevented a crime from occurring.

On top of the tall, brick MCU building, Lieutenant James

Gordon stood next to the Bat-Signal, staring up at the glowing image of the bat.

A young cop named Anna Ramirez stepped onto the roof, carrying a cup of coffee. She handed the cup to Gordon.

"How's your mom?" he asked her, wrapping his fingers around the Styrofoam cup and allowing its warmth to heat his hands.

"Still in the hospital," Ramirez replied solemnly. After a silent moment, she tipped her head at the door leading back into the building. "I was watching TV down below. Mayor announced that you are closing in on the Batman."

Gordon gave a half smile. Some people in Gotham were afraid of Batman, scared because he was taking the law into his own hands. The police had standing orders to arrest him on sight But that was one command Gordon was determined to ignore. He had come to rely on the Caped Crusader, whoever he was, to help the police frighten criminals and keep the city safe.

Detective Ramirez glanced thoughtfully from Lieutenant Gordon to the Bat-Signal. Everyone at MCU knew the Bat-Signal was Gordon's way to call Batman when he needed him. No one talked about it, but it was common knowledge that Gordon had developed an odd sort of friendship with the Batman. Out of respect for Lieutenant Gordon, no one on his team of officers was trying very hard to discover Batman's true identity. On a bulletin board inside, officers had listed possible suspects for who might be wearing the hooded cowl and bullet-proof suit. Their ideas included Elvis Presley, Abraham Lincoln, and the Abominable Snowman.

"Hasn't shown up?" Ramirez asked.

Gordon downed the last of his coffee. "Often doesn't." He crumpled up his cup and prepared to leave the rooftop. "But I like reminding everybody that he's out there."

"Why wouldn't he come?" Detective Ramirez wondered aloud.

"Hopefully," Gordon replied as he flipped off the switch on the Bat-Signal, plunging the sky into complete darkness, "because he's busy."

Two black SUVs and an unmarked white van pulled onto the top floor of a parking garage. A large man climbed out of one of the SUVs. He was a Russian drug lord, known simply as the Chechen.

The Chechen's bodyguard looked around the parking garage nervously. "What if *he* shows up?" the man asked his boss.

"That's why we bring dogs," he replied, speaking to his guard in Russian. "My dogs will take care of the Batman."

The bodyguard opened the back door of the second SUV. Three enormous rottweilers leapt out onto the pavement, growling ferociously. The Chechen bent low and kissed his killer pets.

Then he slowly walked over to the white van, where a man called 'Scarecrow' was waiting for him. They had just begun to talk about how Batman was hurting their business, when suddenly the Chechen's dogs started barking wildly.

"He's here," the bodyguard said uneasily, searching the darkness for any sign of Batman.

"We're all here," a man's voice called out into the night.

Five men in Batman costumes emerged from the shadows. The Batmen were all carrying shotguns.

They never had a chance to fire.

The Chechen's goons were fast and strong. It only took them a few seconds to disarm and capture all five Batmen.

Scarecrow walked over to the prisoners. Their costumes were created from black masks and hockey pads. It didn't take long for him to ferret out the truth. "None of these are the real thing," Scarecrow reported, disgusted.

"How you know?" the Chechen asked.

"Let's just say that me and Batman, well, we're old friends," Scarecrow replied.

Just then, WHAM! A huge, black shape slammed down onto a row of parked cars. It was the Batmobile.

"That's more like it," Scarecrow said with a smile and a nod. "This one's the real deal."

The Chechen's men grabbed their weapons again. They shot at the Batmobile, but their bullets bounced off, sparks flickering in the night like fireflies.

BOOM! The Batmobile's cannons roared into action, surrounding the Chechen's men with blasts of fire. In the chaos Batman, the real Batman, dropped onto the rooftop from his grappling hook.

In a swift move, he freed the fake Batmen, warning them to leave quickly.

"But Batman…" One of the men approached the Caped Crusader, his own flimsy cape waving like a flag in the breeze. "You need us! There's only one of you. It's a war out here!"

Batman didn't reply, he simply pointed to the rooftop exit. Now that the fake Batmen had been freed, there was still

Scarecrow, the Chechen, and his men to take care of.

The five fake Batmen gathered their weapons, adjusted their hockey pads, and disappeared by foot off the rooftop. Batman watched them walk away. He hoped they learned their lesson and would stop trying to 'help.' He didn't have the time to continually rescue weak imitators.

WHOOSH! Batman sprang into action, even though the odds were against him. Moving quickly, keeping to the shadows, Batman leapt and landed solidly between the rows of parked cars with a resounding thud. He fought swiftly, appearing as a whisper in the cool dank air and disappearing as quickly as he'd come. It wasn't long before the Chechen, realizing this was a battle he would not win, called back his dogs and ran away, with his bodyguards scattering into the night. Scarecrow, too, ran off and disappeared.

Leaping into the Batmobile, Batman took off into the city streets. He wasn't going to follow them. Instead he let them run away.

Batman's work here was done. For now.

Chapter Two

On the street in front of Gotham First National Bank, three burglars were loading their guns, checking their equipment, and psyching themselves up for their task. In the basement of the bank, in a highly secured vault, millions of dollars were waiting. Waiting for them to break in and take them.

One of the men slid a clown mask over his face. He looked out from behind the white face, red lips, and bright blue painted smile. His companions were already wearing the exact same masks. This clown adjusted the band around his head, making certain the mask was firmly concealing his true identity, and remarked, "Now we're three of a kind."

Eyeing each other from behind their circus faces, the clowns decided to call themselves Grumpy, Chuckles and Bozo.

"We're it?" Chuckles wondered. "Three guys?" It was, after all, a pretty big job for just three burglars, even with the automatic weapons and hand grenades each man carried.

"There's more on the roof," Grumpy remarked, pointing up above their heads at where two other men in clown masks were sliding silently across a nearby alley along a cable, landing noiselessly onto the bank's rooftop. Lowering his gaze back to where a husky security guard stood just inside the bank, completely unaware of what was about to happen, Grumpy reminded Chuckles that they had to split the money they stole. "Every guy is an extra share. Five shares is plenty."

"Six shares," Bozo cut in, clicking the parts of his weapon into place with a snap and a crack. "Don't forget the guy who planned the job."

Grumpy snorted. "If he thinks he can sit it out and still take a slice of the booty after we're done then I get why they call him 'the Joker.'"

Up on the roof, the two other burglars were working to disarm the bank's security system. They were also discussing the mysterious sixth man, the brains behind the heist.

"Why do they call him the Joker?" Happy asked as he watched Dopey remove screws from an access panel door.

"I heard he wears make-up," Dopey replied.

"Make-up?" Happy asked. He shook his head and gave a small laugh.

"Yeah," Dopey said as the panel slid away revealing a large cluster of wiring and cables. "War paint." Dopey's hands moved quickly across the wiring. It was a matter of seconds before he declared that the alarm was off. "I'm done here," he announced.

"Yes, you are," Happy responded with no emotion in his voice. He quickly attached a silencer to the front of his gun and raised it. No one heard the shot fired. Stepping casually over Dopey's body, Happy grabbed his partner's duffle bag and quickly disappeared though a rooftop doorway into the bank.

CRACK! The sound of gunfire echoed through the main room of Gotham's largest and most prominent bank. Customers began to scream. Tellers ducked behind their booths.

His own gun now drawn, ready for battle, the husky security

guard rushed toward the sound of the gunfire. But the clowns weren't going to be deterred by one lone guard. As Grumpy distracted the man, Chuckles nailed him in the head with the butt of his weapon, hard. The guard slumped to the floor in an unmoving heap.

Grumpy and Bozo gathered the people inside the bank together, handing everyone a hand grenade, then collecting the pins. The hostages were warned that even the slightest movement could cause their grenades to go off. "Obviously, we don't want you doing anything with your hands other than holding on for dear life," Grumpy told them. The frightened hostages huddled together, barely breathing.

Downstairs, Happy worked to open the bank vault. He had to wear his shoes on his hands to protect himself from the electric current coursing through the large metal door.

"They wired this thing with five thousand volts," Happy reported to Grumpy, who had come from upstairs to check on the other clown's progress. "What kind of a bank does that?"

Grumpy knew exactly what kind of bank needed such tight security. "A mob bank," he replied. Then he added, "Guess the Joker's as crazy as they say."

Happy shrugged, continuing to concentrate on opening the vault.

"Where's the alarm guy?" Grumpy asked, realizing that Happy was working alone.

"Boss told me when the guy was done I should take him out. One less clown to share with," Happy responded as the vault door swung open, revealing an eight-foot mountain of cash.

"Funny, he told me something similar." Grumpy lifted his weapon and said goodbye to his fellow clown.

Grumpy strained under the weight of the duffle bags he carried into the bank's lobby. The bags were full and the vault, downstairs was now empty. When he noticed Chuckles' body lifeless nearby, Grumpy strolled past the hostages without even looking at them and straight up to Bozo the clown. Dropping the bags and shoving his pistol into Bozo's back, Grumpy said, "So, you killed Chuckles. I'm betting the Joker told you to kill me off too, as soon as we loaded the cash."

Not at all frightened by Grumpy's weapon in his back, Bozo simply shook his head. "No," he responded. "I kill the bus driver."

Grumpy was confused. "Bus driver? What bus-"

Just then the back of a yellow school bus rammed at top speed through the front window of the bank, glass and brick flying, slamming Grumpy at full force into a teller's window, pinning him to the wall, killing him on impact.

Another clown opened the rear door of the school bus, ready to load the cash on board, but before he even turned away from the door, Bozo shot him. The clown sunk down to the marble bank floor with an audible thud.

Now acting alone, Bozo loaded all the money bags onto the bus himself, closed the door, and climbed into the driver seat.

Police sirens screamed in the distance, but Bozo remained oddly calm, apparently not in a hurry to make his get-a-way. Instead, he took an extra minute to survey the hostages, still clustered together, fearfully clutching their hand grenades.

"I believe what doesn't kill you ...simply makes you stranger." Laughter erupted from the clown, slowly at first, and bubbling up to the point of hysteria when the man whipped off his clown mask, revealing his true identity. He was the Joker, Gotham's newest and most feared criminal mastermind.

Chapter Three

Lieutenant Gordon surveyed the damage at Gotham First National Bank. The hostages had all been rescued, their hand grenades disabled. Officers from MCU were interviewing witnesses, trying to reconstruct what had happened.

Gordon stood in the wreckage at the front of the bank. Shattered glass, bricks, and debris were all that remained of the elaborate entrance. The bodies of five dead men in clown masks had been discovered, one on the roof, one near the empty vault downstairs, and three more in this main area. Forensic specialists were on their way. Gordon expected them to identify the dead men as quickly as possible.

Detective Ramirez approached Gordon as he considered the scene.

"He can't resist showing his face," she told her boss, handing him a series of grainy photographs taken by the bank's security cameras.

Gordon flipped through the images. It was a man's face, but even without the plastic clown mask, he still had the appearance of a circus clown. White pancake make-up, stringy green hair, and a ruby red smile painted over scarred cheeks made him look much more scary than funny.

"Put this out to all police, by morning we can put a big top over central holding and sell tickets," Gordon remarked sarcastically. Then under his breath he wondered, "What's he hiding under that makeup?"

Gordon moved over to Grumpy and reached down, ready to remove the clown's mask. He stopped, instincts alert, as something behind him shifted in the shadows.

Batman.

With a curt nod, Gordon welcomed the intrusion. "Give us a minute people, please!" Gordon called out to Ramirez and the rest of his team. Without questioning the order, the cops all stopped what they were doing and moved away.

Gordon stepped closer to Batman. This was not the time for casual conversation, there were no greetings, Gordon simply thrust the blurry security camera images of the Joker into Batman's gloved hand.

Batman glanced quickly through the pictures, recognizing the villain from other photos that had been taken at smaller heists.

"Him again," Batman handed the pictures back to Gordon. With a tilt of his head, he indicated the fallen bodies of the men in masks. "Who are the others?"

"Another bunch of small-timers," Gordon replied.

Batman reached into his utility belt and pulled out a small tracking devise. He stepped closer to Grumpy's body. PING! The device began flashing and beeping in rapid bursts.

Batman flicked off the tracker and grabbed a stack of money that was lying on the cold floor near Grumpy's outstretched hand. He handed the bundle to Lieutenant Gordon. "These are some of the marked bills I gave you."

When Gordon ran his thumb across the edge of the bills, they fanned, creating a slight stir in the stale air. "My detectives have been busy making drug buys with these for weeks. This bank was another drop for the mob. That makes five banks; we've found the bulk of their dirty cash."

Taking down the mob was part of Batman's grand plan to return Gotham to her glory as a safe and livable city. "Time to move," he said, meaning it was time for Gordon to send cops out into the other banks to confiscate the mob's money, then make arrests.

Gordon was ready. He also wanted the mob brought to their knees, but he had another pressing concern. "What about this Joker guy?" he asked.

"One man or the entire mob?" Batman was certain about what needed to be done. "He can wait."

Agreeing, Gordon began to talk out his plan of action. "We'll have to hit all banks simultaneously. SWAT teams. Back-up. When the new DA gets wind of this, he'll want in."

The District Attorney had recently been elected to office. He'd come from Internal Affairs, where he'd spent his days ferreting out corrupt cops, but that was all Batman knew about the man. "Do you trust him?" Batman asked Gordon directly.

"It would be hard to keep him out," Gordon remarked as he stuffed the bundle of marked bills into an evidence sack. "He's as stubborn as you."

With a smile, Lieutenant Gordon looked up, but the place where Batman had been standing was now empty.

The hiss and rattle of the elevator descending in its shaft did not interrupt Bruce Wayne's focused concentration. There was only one other man in all of Gotham City who knew the location of this concrete bunker, hidden deep underground. Only one other man was party to the secret pathway across the railway bridge, had a key to the rusty padlocked fence, knew where to enter the lopsided abandoned freight container, and understood how to operate the small, shaky elevator.

"It'll be nice when Wayne Manor's rebuilt and you can swap not sleeping in a penthouse for not sleeping in a mansion," Alfred remarked with slight sarcasm as he emerged from the darkness of the elevator, stepping into the artificial light. Alfred placed a thermos in front of Bruce and glanced around.

Ever since Ra's al Ghul had set fire to Wayne Manor, burning the mansion completely to the ground, Bruce had lived in a luxury penthouse in town and worked here in this temporary Bat-Bunker.

In the centre of the low-ceilinged chamber was the Batmobile. Behind the car, Bruce had set up machines that completely covered one wall of the bunker: 3D printers, television screens, and computers.

Images flickered across two of the screens, closed-circuit television news footage of the bank robbery at Gotham National on one screen and a live interview with Harvey Dent, Gotham's new District Attorney, on another.

Bruce Wayne was sitting between the screens, his eyes periodically shifting from one to the other.

Alfred, who had looked after the Wayne family for years, was Bruce's closest confidant and dear friend. "Things are improving. Look at the new District Attorney," Alfred commented, following Bruce's gaze as it settled on the handsome Harvey Dent in a tailored suit.

"I am," Bruce replied. "Closely. I need to know if he can be trusted."

With a press of a button on a nearby control panel,

more images appeared on other screens. Bruce had clearly been following the D.A. for some time. There were videos of the District Attorney at a meeting. Campaigning. Helping someone out of a cab.

Alfred's eyes lingered on this last piece of film. The D.A. was dressed in a blue suit and tie, reaching into an open taxi cab door, guiding a young woman out onto the sidewalk. There was no mistaking the young woman, who was wearing an evening gown, her hair swept up and pinned. Harvey Dent was escorting Bruce's childhood friend, Rachel Dawes, about town.

As Rachel and Harvey Dent disappeared into a restaurant, Alfred gave Bruce a questioning look. "Are you interested in his character…or his social circle?"

Bruce appeared indignant. "Who Rachel spends her time with is her business," he said, ending with a sigh that gave away too much.

Alfred responded lightly, "Well I trust you're not following me on my day off."

Bruce clicked off the screen and the image of Rachel faded into static. "If you ever took one, I might."

Alfred opened the thermos he'd brought and poured Bruce a cup of coffee. He then issued a warning: "Know your limits, Master Wayne."

Bruce stared down into the steaming brew. "Batman has no limits."

Alfred understood all to well. "Ah, but you do, sir."

"I can't afford to know them," Bruce replied.

There was a touch of concern in Alfred's voice as he asked, "What happens the day you find out?"

Bruce turned fully away from his screens and monitors to look Alfred directly in the eyes. "We all know how much you like to say, 'I told you so.'"

Alfred evenly met his young charge's gaze. "That day, Master Wayne, even I won't want to." Breaking away, he headed back to the elevator, muttering under his breath as he pressed the button to take him back up into the railway yard, "Probably."

Chapter Four

Rachel Dawes, Assistant District Attorney, had just witnessed the most amazing thing. At a trial to convict the mob boss Sal Maroni, one of Maroni's goons was the witness for the prosecution. But he refused to finger his boss, instead pulling a gun on District Attorney Harvey Dent.

If it wasn't for a coin toss, Rachel would have been the one interviewing the man. It would have been her facing the barrel of that weapon.

When Harvey had arrived late to the courtroom, she'd suggested that maybe she should question the witness. In response, Dent had pulled a large silver dollar out of his pocket and flashed it at her.

"You're flipping coins to see who leads?" Rachel asked, incredulous.

Dent smiled fondly at her, "It's my father's lucky coin. As I recall, it got me my first date with you."

He flipped his coin into the air. Heads, he'd take on the witness. Tails, Rachel would lead.

The coin spun. Rachel didn't see anything humorous in using a coin toss to make an important decision. "I'm serious, Harvey," she told him. "You don't leave things like this to chance."

He caught the dollar and pressed it into the back of his left hand. Heads.

"I don't," he told her with full sincerity as he prepared to take on the witness. "I make my own luck." Dent tucked his coin back into his pocket.

And he had been lucky indeed. The witness's gun had misfired and a bullet had whizzed right by the D.A.'s ear.

Rachel was glad she hadn't been the one to dodge the bullet. She wouldn't have known how to respond, but Harvey Dent had not been phased in the least by the incident. He stepped forward and snagged the gun from the man in a single, quick, smooth move. Then Harvey Dent punched the witness with a swift right cross to the jaw.

The downside to the whole affair was that Sal Maroni went free, but in Rachel's opinion the fact that the mob was shooting at the D.A. meant something positive. It was a sure sign that the mob was under pressure. The mob was scared of Harvey Dent.

"I'm fine, by the way," Dent interrupted, as Rachel jabbered on and on excitedly about how the mob had tried to kill him.

Rachel grinned at Harvey, reaching up to straighten his jacket lapels with great admiration. "You're Gotham's D.A.," she told him. "If you aren't getting shot at, you're not doing your job." She smiled. "Why don't we take the rest of the day off?"

"Can't," Dent replied, stalling her hands by placing his own over them. "I dragged the head of the Major Crimes Unit down here."

"Jim Gordon?" Rachel asked, remembering the night, not so long ago, that Lieutenant Gordon had saved her life. "He's a friend," she told Harvey, gathering her jacket, preparing to return to her own office. She was nearly out the door when, knowing that the relationship between Lieutenant Gordon and

Dent was strained, she added, "Try to be nice."

"I want to meet him," Dent said to Gordon, immediately after the Lieutenant entered the D.A.'s office.

Taking a seat opposite Dent, Gordon looked blankly at the D.A. as if he didn't know who Dent was talking about.

Dent tossed a bundle of cash recovered from the Joker's bank heist onto his desk. "Lightly irradiated bills. Fancy stuff for a city cop." Dent clearly knew Gordon had help obtaining marked bills to circulate among the mob's drug dealers.

"We liaise with various agencies-" Gordon replied, picking up the bills and avoiding Dent's gaze.

"Save it, Gordon," Dent wasn't buying his act. He knew who'd been providing the money. "When can I meet him?"

Gordon shrugged. "Official policy is to arrest the vigilante known as Batman on sight." It was, after all, Harvey Dent's own rule.

Dent didn't appreciate Gordon's refusal to set up a meeting. He battled back, verbally attacking Gordon's leadership of MCU. "I don't like that you've got your own *special* unit, and I don't like that it's full of cops I investigated at Internal Affairs."

Gordon didn't engage. Deep down, he knew that Dent was probably right. There might be a couple of bad cops in his ranks, but there wasn't a whole lot he could do about it. "If I didn't work with cops you'd investigated while you were making your name at Internal Affairs," Gordon told Dent, "I'd be working alone. I have to do the best I can with what I have."

Gordon moved on to the business at hand. "I need those

search warrants for my ongoing investigation."

Dent wasn't so sure. "You want me to back warrants for five banks without telling me who we are after?"

"In this town, the fewer people who know about something, the safer the operation," Gordon explained. "I can give you the names of the banks."

"Well that's a start." Dent pushed the marked bills to the side of his desk and pulled some papers from a drawer. "I'll get you your warrants. But I want your trust." He caught Gordon's eyes with his own.

Lieutenant Gordon got up from the chair. "You don't have to sell me, Dent. We all know you're Gotham's White Knight."

Dent grinned. "I hear they have a different nickname for me down at MCU."

Not a very nice one, Gordon thought to himself. But to Dent, he simply smiled.

Chapter Five

In the spacious, tastefully decorated board room of Wayne Enterprises, three men had gathered for an important business meeting.

"Mr. Fox," Lau, the Chinese CEO of L.S. I. Holdings, opened the meeting. Lau had travelled all the way from Hong Kong to speak to Lucius Fox, his counterpart at Wayne Enterprises, and Bruce Wayne, majority shareholder in Gotham's most prominent business. "In China, L.S.I. Holdings stands for dynamic new growth. A joint Chinese venture with Wayne Enterprises will be a powerhouse," Lau began.

Lucius Fox had worked for the Wayne family for many years. He'd been down in Applied Sciences developing new and exciting industry prototypes when Bruce took over the leadership of the company. Bruce had quickly promoted the quiet and unassuming man to the CEO position. Fox knew about Bruce's alter ego as Batman. He was the one who'd provided the Batsuit, its shape-changing cape, and, most importantly, the Batmobile, but Fox kept that information tucked in the back recess of his mind, never exactly admitting the truth.

Fox bowed slightly, as was Chinese custom, saying, "Well, Mr. Lau, I speak for the rest of the board, and Mr. Wayne here, in expressing our own excitement…" his voice trailed off as the two men simultaneously turned to look at the third person at the morning meeting.

With his head resting comfortably on the board room's marble-topped conference table, Bruce Wayne was sound asleep.

Offering no apology for his boss's behaviour, Fox walked Lau to the elevator, telling him that they would be in touch to further their business negotiations. As the elevator doors closed, Fox was approached by Mr. Reese, an ambitious lawyer helping with the deal.

"Here are the numbers you wanted, Mr. Fox," Reese said, holding out a stack of papers. "I have reviewed L.S.I. Holdings' accounting numbers for you."

"Did you find anything unusual?" Fox asked, eyeing the papers, but not taking them.

"Nothing," Reese replied.

"Hmmm," Fox said, thoughtfully. "I have a bad feeling. There is something suspicious about Chairman Lau. Run them again, Mr. Reese."

Returning to the board room, Fox discovered Bruce was awake, standing by the large window.

"Another long night?" Fox asked, hinting that he knew a little about what Bruce Wayne did by night.

Bruce merely smiled.

Fox came to stand next to Bruce at the window. He looked out over the city, soaking in the view. "This joint venture was your idea. The consultants love it. But I'm not convinced," Fox said as he rotated on a heel to face Bruce. "L.S.I.'s grown eight percent annually, like clockwork. They must have a revenue stream that's off the books. Maybe even illegal."

"Okay," Bruce was one step ahead of his CEO. "Cancel the

deal."

Fox leaned in, looking closely at Mr. Wayne's face, trying to better read the man. "You already knew," Fox declared, seeing a trace of a grin curling the edges of Bruce's lips.

Bruce shrugged. "Pretending to work a business deal was the only way I could get close to Lau. I wanted a good look at their books."

Fox gave Bruce a wry stare and asked sarcastically, "Anything else you can trouble me for?"

Bruce knew it was a joke, but he responded as if it was a serious request. "I need a new suit."

Looking him over head to toe, Fox responded, "Three buttons *is* a little nineties."

Bruce looked down at his hand-tailored suit and straightened his tie. "I'm not talking about fashion, Mr. Fox, so much as function."

Bruce reached into his coat pocket and pulled out some sketches. Fox laid them on the board room table, slipped on his reading glasses, and looked them over. "You want to be able to turn your head?" he asked.

This time Bruce made the joke. "Sure would make backing out of the driveway easier."

Fox took the sketches and stuffed them in his own pocket, saying, "I'll see what I can do."

"Do you think this suit is outdated?" Bruce Wayne asked his date as he held the restaurant's door open for her. He was wearing the same suit from the meeting with Lau earlier in the day.

Natascha glanced at the suit and shrugged. She wasn't a

fashion expert. She was a prima ballerina with the Moscow Ballet. In lieu of an answer, she took Bruce's arm and held it tightly, leaning into him slightly while they entered the restaurant.

This was Gotham's latest hotspot. Reservations were impossible to get. There was a three month wait list, unless of course you were Bruce Wayne. He owned the place.

Natascha didn't know it, but good food wasn't the only reason they'd come to this particular restaurant tonight. Bruce had information that Rachel was here, right now, with Harvey Dent. He had been planning all along to crash their date. Steering Natascha to the right, he approached the table where Rachel and Dent were reviewing their menus.

He acted as if the meeting had been a coincidence. "Rachel." He leaned over to kiss her briefly on the cheek. "Fancy that."

Rachel could see through Bruce's farce. She'd known him her whole life. "Yes, Bruce," she replied rolling her eyes. "Fancy that."

Bruce introduced Natascha, forcing Rachel to introduce her date as well. This was the reason he'd come, Bruce reminded himself. Not to check on Rachel, but to meet and size up Harvey Dent.

"The infamous playboy Bruce Wayne," Dent rose to shake hands with Bruce. "Rachel's told me everything about you."

Bruce couldn't help from responding with a smile. "I certainly hope not." Knowing it would bother Rachel didn't stop him from suggesting they combine tables and have dinner together. There was so much about Harvey Dent that Bruce wanted to find out. Things that Batman needed to confirm.

While Rachel talked to Natascha about the Moscow ballet, Harvey and Bruce talked about Dent's personal mission to clean up Gotham City. Bruce was impressed by the man's passion.

"I guess you either die a hero or you live long enough to see yourself become the villain," Dent told Bruce. "Look, whoever this Batman is, he doesn't want to spend the rest of his life doing this. How could he? Batman's looking for someone else to take up his mantle."

It was too true, Bruce thought to himself. He hoped that Harvey Dent was the face Gotham needed.

Natascha jumped into the conversation. "Someone like you maybe, Mr. Dent?"

Dent leaned back in his chair, crossing his arms across his chest. "Maybe," he replied. "If I'm up to it."

Bruce liked Dent's response. He had begun to consider the possibility that Batman could pass the job of cleaning up Gotham to someone else. If Harvey Dent was going to take on that role, Bruce knew he'd need to secure the man's position as D.A.

New elections weren't for another three years, but he could get Harvey the money he'd need to win that election and any others he might have in his future. Bruce offered to have a party for Harvey, a fundraiser. "After an evening with my friends," Bruce explained, "you'll never need another fundraiser."

It was an invitation Harvey Dent could not refuse.

Chapter Six

In the heavily guarded conference room of a downtown hotel, not too far from where Bruce Wayne was dining with Harvey Dent, Gotham's mob was gathering. The Chechen, the mob boss Sal Maroni, and a thin African-American gangster named Gambol were sitting around a table. Each man had his own bodyguards in attendance. To avoid trouble between themselves, they'd left their weapons at the door. There had never been a meeting of Gotham's underground leadership before tonight.

The men eyed each other warily before turning their attention to the television in the centre of the table.

Onscreen was Lau, sitting in a high-backed chair, addressing the group live from an undisclosed location.

"As you are all aware," Lau told the gangsters, "one of our deposits was stolen. A relatively small amount – sixty-eight million dollars." He was referring to the robbery from Gotham First National Bank.

The Chechen's strong Russian accent became even stronger when he angrily blurted out, "Who is stupid enough to steal from us?"

Lau replied, "I'm told the man who arranged the heist calls himself the Joker."

"Who is he?" The Chechen demanded to know.

Sal Maroni told the big Russian to calm himself. He knew all about the Joker. "He's a two-bit whack job, wears a cheap purple suit and make-up," Maroni explained. "He's not the problem. He's a nobody." Maroni looked at Lau on the TV and said, "The problem is our money is being tracked by the cops."

Murmurs of surprise swept the room. This was the first time in Gotham's history the mob's money had been tracked by the police.

Lau tilted his head at Maroni. "Thanks to information passed to us from Mr. Maroni's crooked cops at MCU, we know the police have indeed identified our banks using marked bills and are planning to seize the rest of our funds today."

Lau told them that the D.A. had given Lieutenant Gordon search warrants for all five of the banks holding mob money. That very minute, Gordon and his SWAT team were preparing to enter the five banks simultaneously.

"We need to move the money to another location," Lau suggested. "Outside of Gotham. Somewhere it will be safe from the Gotham police. I believe Hong Kong is our best option."

The gangsters protested. No one wanted the mob's money to leave Gotham. It was their money. They liked to live rich and used that cash to fuel more illegal activities, making them even richer.

As the men argued, unable to trust each other or decide how best to handle their problems with the police, a roar of laughter sounded from the very back of the conference room. The laughter grew, and grew, until it filled the room completely.

The arguing ceased. All eyes turned to a dark corner of the room.

With no flourish or fanfare, just the sound of crazy laughter leading the way, the Joker came into view. His scarred cheeks were carved into a permanent smile. Sweaty clown makeup was smeared over his face, blanching his skin into a grayish-white hue. Red-painted lips surrounded a crazed grin. If his maniacal laughter hadn't silenced the crowd, his appearance would have.

Gambol glanced over at his bodyguard. "Give me one reason I shouldn't have my boy here pull your head off."

The Joker stopped laughing and replied, "I know you are afraid to go out at night. Batman has shown Gotham your true colours. And Dent's just beginning to get in on the hero act." The Joker grinned at Lau onscreen and continued, "As for his so-called-plan to move the money to Hong Kong – city, state, or country borders won't stop Batman. He has no jurisdiction." The Joker pointed directly at Lau. "Batman will find him and make him squeal."

"What do you propose?" The Chechen asked.

"It's simple," the Joker replied. "Kill the Batman."

The mobsters in the room began to snicker. "If it's so easy, why haven't you done it already?" Sal Maroni asked the Joker.

"Like my mother used to tell me – if you're good at something, never do it for free." The Joker rubbed his hands together with glee. He was about to make the mob a proposition.

"How much you want?" The Chechen's accent was getting stronger again, as his temper rose.

"Half."

The gangsters stared at the Joker. They couldn't believe he wanted half. Half of all the money they'd worked so hard to acquire? Gambol spoke up. "Maybe we should just kill you instead?"

The Joker responded by opening his jacket to reveal a bomb strapped to his chest. If they tried to kill him, he'd take them with him.

"Let me know when you change your mind," the Joker said, strolling casually out of the room.

When he was gone, Maroni turned to Lau. It was now important that they protect their money, not just from the police, but from the Joker as well. "How soon can you move the money?"

Lau smiled tightly. "I already have," he informed the leaders of Gotham's mob. The camera pulled out to reveal that Lau was sitting on an airplane. With the rumble of an engine, the plane lifted off. Lau had stolen all the mob's money.

The mob members, furious that their money was gone, erupted into angry shouts. Elsewhere, Lieutenant Gordon was also furious; his SWAT teams had entered five different Gotham City banks and were all reporting the same thing: The vaults were completely empty.

Chapter Seven

High on the roof of the MCU, the Bat-Signal illuminated the evening sky. This time, Batman heeded the call and landed softly with his wings outstretched. He expected to find Lieutenant Gordon standing there, prepared to report about the SWAT raid on the mob's money. The man who faced Batman was not Gordon, but rather Harvey Dent.

"You're a hard man to reach," Dent said as he stepped fully into the light of the Bat-Signal. Dent would have continued if the rooftop door hadn't suddenly swung open with a resounding crash.

Weapon drawn, Gordon burst onto the roof, ready to fire at whoever was messing with his signal. Discovering that it was Dent who had called Batman did not put a smile on Gordon's face, but it did force him to lower his weapon. Stone-faced, he joined the conversation.

"Lau's halfway to Hong Kong," Dent told Gordon. "If you'd only asked, I could have taken his passport. I told you to keep me in the loop."

Gordon, tucking his gun into his holster, responded, "Yeah? All that was left in the vaults were the marked bills. They knew we were coming. As soon as your office got involved, there's a leak…"

Dent was indignant. "My office? You're sitting down there with scum like Detectives Wuertz and Ramirez-" Dent's voice trailed off as Batman stepped closer to the two men. Now was not the time to argue about whether Gordon had a couple of crooked cops on his team. The leak could have come from anywhere.

Turning to Batman, Dent said, "We need Lau back, but the Chinese won't extradite a national under any circumstances."

Batman considered the situation. "If I get him to you, can you get him to talk?"

Dent nodded confidently, "I'll get him to sing."

Gordon piped in. "If we're going after the mob's life savings, things will get ugly." It was a subtle warning to Dent that his life might on the line.

"I knew the risks when I took this job, Lieutenant," Dent said firmly. "Same as you." Then, looking back toward Batman, Dent asked, "How will you get him back, anyways?" Dent's question hung in the air. Batman had already disappeared. With a surprised expression, Dent looked at Gordon.

Gordon smirked and said with a shrug, "He does that."

Bruce Wayne found Lucius Fox down in the basement of Wayne Enterprises, in the Applied Sciences lab. Fox was hard at work redesigning the new "suit" Bruce had requested. Bruce let Lucius lead him to a highly secured cabinet, double and triple locked for protection. After twisting various knobs and pressing secret buttons, Lucius opened the door to reveal what his boss had ordered.

Bruce was awed as he looked over the armoured plating secured to mesh fabric.

Fox explained to Bruce how the Batsuit was made. "Hardened Kevlar plates on a titanium dipped fibre, tri-weaved for flexibility." Bruce smiled and Fox added, "You'll be lighter, faster, more agile." Fox paused. "Now, there's a trade-off. The spread of the plates gives you weak spots. You'll be more vulnerable to gunfire and knives."

"We wouldn't want things getting too easy, would we?" Bruce responded dryly, but even Fox could see that Bruce was thrilled. This Batsuit, flaws and all, was exactly what he'd been hoping for. He lifted one of the suit's arms. There were new double-blade scallops on the gauntlet. Nice!

Bruce wondered what the little black button on the side did...

WHOOSH! Fox ducked as one of the blades on the gauntlet suddenly fired. From within the arm plate, three spinning disks had shot out, whipping through the air like a ninja's throwing stars and nearly missing Bruce's ear. The Batarangs slammed into a filing cabinet more than halfway across the room, embedding themselves in the hard metal.

Fox looked at Bruce with a mixture of amusement and horror. "Perhaps you should read the instructions first."

Bruce blushed, his face hot with embarrassment. "Sorry," he muttered.

Fox planned to send the suit to the Bat-Bunker, but for now he set the black armour plates and gauntlets back in the cabinet and locked the door. As he reset the alarms Fox said, "Our Chinese friend left town before I could tell him the deal was off."

Bruce put his arm on Fox's shoulder. "I'm sure you've always wanted to go to Hong Kong." Fox knew Bruce wasn't offering him a nice vacation.

"What's wrong with a phone call?" Fox asked, shaking

his head.

"I think Mr. Lau deserves a more personal touch." Bruce winked, then guided Fox over to a table in the centre of the vast Applied Sciences lab. There he showed Lucius a detailed plan for their trip to Hong Kong. To make the plan work, the first thing they needed was a very special kind of airplane.

Luckily for Bruce Wayne, Lucius Fox knew exactly where to get one.

Chapter Eight

From the cargo hold of a four-engine turboprop aircraft, Bruce Wayne was slipping into his parachute, preparing to jump. His face was covered by a black balaclava and he was wearing a flight suit to conceal his street clothes. Covered head to toe in fatigues, Bruce Wayne looked like any other military airman.

Bruce was ready, anxious for word that the airplane was in position over Hong Kong. The co-pilot rotated in his seat and gave Bruce a thumbs-up. Bruce fixed an oxygen mask over his face and, without a moment's hesitation, leapt out the craft.

He soared lower and lower until, at the last possible minute, he opened his chute, hoping he'd gone beneath the city's radar and would be landing undetected. The winds did him a favour, pushing him close to the water's edge in the final seconds, right on target.

Dragging himself from the harbour, Bruce ditched his chute and wet jumpsuit and hurried past the freeway overpass to a nearby escalator.

Reaching his destination, a narrow bridge overlooking the harbour, Bruce blended into the crowd like any other tourist, raising a camera and taking pictures of the beautiful city skyline.

Another tourist stood a few feet away, carefully studying a map.

The tourist with the map approached Bruce with unguarded

familiarity. "There's a better view from the peak tram," he suggested.

It was Fox.

Bruce feigned interest in Fox's map, pointing at one specific building in the centre of town. "So," he asked, "how's the view from L.S.I. Holdings?"

Fox joked that the tram was better for tourists like themselves. "L.S. I. is restricted," he informed Bruce. "Lau's holed up there good and tight."

Continuing to appear as if he were pouring over a travel map, Fox told Bruce about his morning visit to see Lau at L.S.I.

Fox had arrived by private helicopter, courtesy of L.S.I. Holdings, to the rooftop of the Peninsula Hotel. Lau did not meet him personally. Instead, two Chinese businessmen collected Fox at the helipad and ushered him inside.

"I'm afraid for security reasons I have to ask for your mobile phone," a security guard sitting behind a clean, white counter requested.

Lucius handed over his phone freely, watching carefully as the guard stashed it in a box underneath the desk.

The business men led Fox into his breakfast meeting with Lau. The dining room was stunning. Huge plate glass windows encircled the two men, providing breathtaking views of Hong Kong and the rising sun.

Lau rose as Fox entered the room. "I apologize for leaving Gotham in the middle of our negotiations," he said, indicating that Fox should be seated. With the crook of a finger he signalled a waiter to pour his guest a glass of juice. "A businessman of your stature will understand. But with you here…we can continue."

Fox took a sip of the juice. "Well, it was good of you to bring me out here in such style, Mr. Lau, but I've actually come-" Brrrinnng. Brrrinnng. The ringing of a cell phone cut Fox's statement short. From his pocket, Fox pulled out a second cell phone, identical to the one he'd left at security. He switched off the ringer, apologizing for the intrusion.

"We do not allow cell phones in here," Lau looked at the phone, now lying by Fox's plate, with disgust.

"Forgot I had it." Fox simply shrugged. "So, I've come to explain why we're going to have to put our deal on hold."

Upon hearing the unexpected news, Lau stared at Fox, red-faced and fuming.

When he was done explaining the situation to Lau, Fox rose from the table, collecting his cell phone as he stood. "We at Wayne Enterprises can't afford to be seen doing business with…" he paused, searching for the right descriptive words and finding none, and continued, "Well, whatever it is you're accused of being. A businessman of your stature will understand."

Lau jumped up from the table, anger shining in his eyes.

Lucius walked away without turning back. At the security desk, the guard offered him back his phone. Fox merely smiled, shaking his head, and held up the duplicate phone. The security guard looked momentarily confused, then placed Lucius's cell phone back in the box under the desk.

Now on the pedestrian walkway of the bridge, Fox showed Bruce the phone he had carried into his meeting with Lau.

Running a finger over the touch screen, a 3D map of Lau's office suite popped up. Bruce took the phone from Fox, completely impressed.

"What's this?" Bruce asked, turning it over in his hands, contemplating the many uses of such an amazing device.

"I had R and D work it up," Fox said modestly. "It sends out high frequencies and records the response time to map an environment."

Bruce couldn't help but smile. "Sonar. Just like a ba-"

"Submarine," Fox interjected quickly, cutting Bruce off. "Like a submarine."

Bruce gave a quick chuckle. He knew more about sonar than most. It occurred to him to ask Fox where the transmitting device was, but then he realized the other phone, the one that Fox had left in the security guard's box, was sending the signal. Excited about the implications of such technology, Bruce's head was full of ideas for future applications as he thanked Lucius and began to move off into the crush of Hong Kong life.

"Mr. Wayne?" Fox called after him just before he disappeared altogether.

Bruce turned back.

"Good luck."

In the darkness shortly before dawn, Batman crouched on the rooftop of a building directly across from L.S.I. Holdings. The blades of his gauntlets were clicked in place and his utility belt was filled with the equipment he required for tonight's mission. The new suit moved comfortably, like a second skin, and the redesigned cowl allowed him the freedom to turn his head with greater ease.

Still, he took things slowly. With small, precise movements, he stood gradually, careful to remain undetected by the security camera, red light glowing, just above his head. The mission would have to be aborted if he were discovered.

Batman pulled two black boxes from his belt and snapped them together to create a high-powered scope on a rifle-like device.

There! He spotted his target. Slightly below where he stood was the office window of Chairman Lau. Batman fired the scope/rifle four times. With each silenced explosion, a sticky bomb shot out, attaching itself to the glass of the L.S.I. building. Peering through the scope again, Batman checked that the timers on each sticky bomb had been activated. They were counting down the minutes. Now, he had to move quickly.

Inside L.S.I Holdings' offices, the phone Fox had left behind glowed blue in the box under the desk. Suddenly, all of the building's lights went out and, in the exact same moment, all of the security doors unlocked and flung themselves open.

The telephone in Lau's hand went dead. Filled with impending dread, Lau pulled out a handgun from his desk and rushed wildly into the hall screaming in Chinese, "Where are the police? What am I paying them for?"

With a leap into the vast space between the two buildings, Batman swooped off the taller building, activating the special fabric in his cape. Acting like wings, it slowed his descent and allowing him to change course, streaking around the other building's side, floating toward a large window in the rear.

In a single movement, combining a SHOOSH and a WHAM, Batman quickly collapsed his cape, gathered it around himself, and hurled through the window.

The police had already arrived. Batman could hear the ding of the elevator bells, the stomping of footsteps echoing in the stairwells, and dispatch radios barking out commands.

Hustling toward Lau's office, Batman mused that he would be long gone before they even got close.

Lau's office door was locked. Batman correctly guessed that the man was cowering inside, gripping his shotgun as if it were his lifeline.

SLAM! Batman kicked in the door, careful to be out of the way when Lau fired at the sound of intrusion. In the light of Lau's gunbursts, Batman swooped down on Lau before the man could even identify who had knocked in his door. In a lightning fast move, Batman attached a small pack to Lau's back, and then, just as he'd planned, the timers on Batman's four sticky bombs ticked down to zero.

The police burst into the office, just as the wall and ceiling behind Lau and Batman exploded, revealing the dawn sky breaking above Hong Kong. Batman quickly pulled the ripcord on Lau's pack. A weather balloon emerged from the pack, filling itself with helium. Lau began to laugh. The balloon floated gently two hundred feet up, attached to him by a thin thread of high-test nylon. It looked like a mismatched fight, Batman's balloon versus the entire Hong Kong Police force and their automatic weapons.

A low rumble filled the room. Curious, the police held their weapons trained on the human bat, but didn't fire.

The rumble was becoming louder and louder.

How quickly the tables turned. One minute Lau was laughing at his good fortune, the next, the thread from his weather balloon pack was caught up in the V-shaped nose of a massive, soaring, C-130 aircraft. This was the plane Bruce Wayne had asked Lucius to find.

Lau and Batman were yanked from the building and carried off into the glowing, orange and yellow sunrise.

Lau's scream echoed long after he was gone.

Lieutenant Gordon was in his office at MCU looking through case files when Detective Ramirez walked in.

"You're gonna want to see this," she told Gordon, directing his attention outside the window to a place on the lawn where a crowd was forming.

Gordon hurried down the stairs, burst out the door, and pressed his way through to the centre of the gathering.

On the ground, trussed like a chicken, was Lau. A sign taped to his chest read: Please deliver to Lieutenant Gordon.

A few paces away, the media was interviewing Harvey Dent about Lau's miraculous reappearance.

"By taking Lau out of Hong Kong, the Chinese government claims its international rights have been broken." The reporter thrust his microphone into Dent's face. "How do you respond?"

Dent grinned, leaning into the microphone and relishing the moment. "I don't know about Mr. Lau's travel arrangements," he said with a small laugh. "But I'm sure glad he's back."

Chapter Nine

The D.A. had a plan. If Lau would give them damaging information about the mob, they could charge all of Gotham's mobsters under the R.I.C.O. Act as one criminal. According to the Racketeer Influenced and Corrupt Organization Act, if it could be proven that the mobsters were somehow linked, they would all go down together.

Lau knew the information necessary to close down Gotham's underworld once and for all.

He and Dent made a deal. In exchange for the information necessary to engage the R.I.C.O. Act, Lau would eventually be given exactly what he wanted; immunity, protection, and a chartered plane back to Hong Kong. They also agreed that Lau would stay at MCU, where Gordon could keep an eye on him, rather than at the county holding facility.

Within the hour, SWAT teams were dispatched throughout Gotham City, and the police had descended on and nabbed five hundred and forty-nine of the mob's nastiest thugs, including Sal Maroni.

The criminals arrived, not one by one, but by an over-crowded bus load to the courtroom of Judge Surrillo at Gotham Municipal Court.

Paperwork took over her desk in thick stacks. With more than five hundred defendants, people were squeezed into every nook and cranny of the courtroom.

Judge Surrillo called order, then read the charges. "Eight

hundred forty-nine counts racketeering. Two hundred forty-six counts fraud. Eighty-seven counts conspiracy murder-" She was flipping through the pages, looking for additional charges to add to the heap, when a playing card slid out from between two documents.

The judge considered it momentarily but didn't have the time to guess how it got there, or what it meant. She picked up the card, turning it once in her hand, then moved it to the side, thinking how ironic it was that her courtroom was like a circus and the playing card was a clown – the joker. Decidedly setting the card aside, she called for order once again, before continuing the trial.

"The public likes you, Dent," Gotham's mayor told the D.A in the Mayor's office, across the street from Judge Surillo's chaotic courtroom. "That's the only reason this might fly."

Mayor Garcia pursed his lips and gazed hard at Harvey Dent. "They're all coming after you, now," he warned. "Not just the mob...politicians, journalists, cops – anyone whose wallet is about to get lighter without the mob's money in the hidden lining." Dent didn't blink against the Mayor's unwavering stare. "Are you up to it?" Dent gave a terse nod in agreement. He was ready for anything that might come at him. "You better be. If they get anything on you...those criminals will be back on the streets."

The Mayor broke their stare-down, stepped over to the window, and looked outside, adding in soft undertones, "Followed swiftly by you and me-"

BANG! A dark shape cracked the glass in front of the

Mayor's office.

Stepping quickly in front of the mayor, Dent moved to protect him, both men fearful of an assassination attempt.

"It's Batman," Dent flatly informed the Mayor, staring with disbelief at the limp body that had hit the mayor's window. The body was hanging by its neck from the municipal flag pole, cape loosely billowing in the wind. But wait! There was something odd about the dead man. Beneath his cowl, his mouth was strangely deformed, cut and bloody, and painted in a demonic clown smile.

Dent rushed outside to get a closer look.

Not Batman, he assured himself. He watched as police struggled to bring the thin, short body down off the flagpole. Dent had met Batman and this wasn't him, he thought in relief. He's a fake.

Dent moved in to see the body which had now been laid out on the lawn. Lieutenant Gordon, ever-present when a crime had been committed, was already on the scene.

A card was pinned to the imitation batsuit with a knife.

Another joker.

Gordon leaned forward, reading the hand-written note on the playing card aloud: "Will the real Batman please reveal himself?

In Bruce Wayne's plush penthouse, Alfred was busy overseeing the decorations for that evening's party, the fundraiser for Harvey Dent.

"How's it going?" Bruce asked Alfred, coming in to inspect the buffet table, already laden with breads and cheeses and other appetizers. The first guests would begin arriving any moment.

"I think your fundraiser will be a great success, sir," Alfred said with a sly smile. He was convinced that Bruce's real motive for throwing this party was to see Rachel. No matter how Bruce protested, Alfred didn't believe him.

"It's not true," Bruce said in response to Alfred's suspicious expression. He would have continued to defend his reasons for the bash if an image on the continuously streaming TV news hadn't caught his eye.

Across the bottom of the screen, in a bright bold font, read the words: Is Batman Dead?

An image of a fake Batman hanging dead from the flagpole filled the screen. Bruce hurried to the television set to run up the volume.

Mike Engel, a Gotham TV reporter, was anchoring the story. "Police have released video footage found concealed on the body." Engel warned, "Sensitive viewers beware: the images you are about to see are disturbing."

The image shifted to the fake Batman, clearly in the hours before his death, blindfolded, and held in a non-descript room.

The Joker was in the room with him. Standing beside the fake Batman, his gruesome face was stuck as always in its horrific smile. Looking straight at the camera, the Joker declared, "You want order in Gotham? Batman has to go." He leaned in to the screen, his disturbingly comical face filling the picture. "Batman must take off his mask and turn himself in. Every day he doesn't, people will die. Starting tonight. I am a man of my word."

The tape faded to static and Bruce immediately understood the rest of the story. Engel cut back to an image of the fake

Batman's lifeless body swinging by a rope.

Bruce clicked off the television and sank back into his couch, disturbed and pensive, considering how best to respond.

Chapter Ten

At MCU, Detective Ramirez had to hurry to catch up to Lieutenant Gordon. She was carrying paperwork that he needed to see.

Gordon didn't stop his forward progress, but thrust out his hand behind to take the papers, as if in a relay race, and have a quick look on the go. He perused the lab's findings while Ramirez explained, "That joker card, pinned to the body? Forensics found three sets of prints on it."

Gordon was surprised at this news. There had been no fingerprints discovered at the scenes of any crimes where they'd encountered the Joker previously. "Any matches?" he asked, hopeful.

"All three," Ramirez told him.

Gordon stopped solidly in his tracks. He spun to face her, eager to hear the rest.

"They belong to Judge Surrillo, Harvey Dent, and Commissioner Loeb," Ramirez replied.

This was not what Gordon had hoped to hear. The matches weren't for the Joker at all, but for his future victims. "The Joker is telling us who he's targeting," Gordon knew with unwavering certainty. He shook his head to clear it. They were going to have to act fast to prevent any further deaths tonight. He barked orders at Ramirez. "Get a unit to Surrillo's house. Tell Wuertz to find Dent. Get them both into protective custody." His head practically spun around as he surveyed the police working quietly at their desks in MCU. It was the calm before the storm. "Where's the commissioner?"

"City Hall."

Gordon nodded at Ramirez. "Seal the building. No one in or out till I get there."

Across town, on the stoop in front of Judge Surrillo's brownstone, the Judge was questioning the two uniformed police officers who had rung her doorbell.

"Gordon wants me to go right now?" she asked, noting the late hour.

"These are dangerous people, Judge," one of the men told her, guiding her out of her house and down into the street. "Even we don't know where you are going." At the curb, he handed her a sealed envelope and then stepped aside, letting her settle into the driver's seat of her sedan.

"Before you start the engine you are supposed to open the envelope," the other cop explained. "It'll tell you where you are going."

Trusting that these two men really were officers sent by Lieutenant Gordon, Judge Surrillo did exactly as they told her.

From the seat in her car, Judge Surrillo watched the officers drive away. Anxious to discover her destination, she ripped open the envelope and pulled out the sheet of paper. There was only one word on it: "UP"

Not a second later, her car exploded, heaving upward in a massive fireball.

In a nearby alley, a passerby was thrown to the ground by the force of the eruption. Burning debris fluttered all around him. He raised a fragment. The shards of paper in the air were singed playing cards.

Nothing but jokers.

Lieutenant Gordon entered City Hall through tight security at the front door. It was easy to find Commissioner Loeb. He was completely surrounded by armed cops. And he didn't look at all happy about it.

"Gordon, what are you playing at?" Loeb shouted across the room at Gordon before the Lieutenant had a chance to approach.

Security at the forefront of his mind, Lieutenant Gordon first checked that the windows were locked, then told his men. "We're secure." He instructed the officers to do a floor by floor search of the building.

Finally, Gordon turned to address Commissioner Loeb. "I'm sorry, sir. We believe the Joker has made a threat against your life."

Loeb didn't appear concerned. "Take my word for it –the Police Commissioner earns a lot of threats." With large, purposeful strides, Loeb and Gordon headed into Loeb's office. There Commissioner Loeb beelined for his desk drawer and pulled out a tumbler glass and a bottle of whiskey. "I found the appropriate response to these situations a long time ago…" His voice trailed off as he poured himself a drink. "You get to explain to my wife why I'm late for dinner, Lieutenant." Loeb screwed the lid back on the bottle and swirled the soft bronze liquid in his glass.

Gordon felt that Loeb was being much too cavalier about the situation. "Sir," he began in earnest, "the joker card pinned to the fake Batman had your fingerprint on it."

Loeb lifted his glass beneath his nose and sniffed the pungent brew. "How'd they get my print?" Loeb wondered aloud before tilting back his head and taking a large gulp of whiskey.

"Somebody with access to your house or office must've lifted it off a tissue or a glass," Gordon said, staring into the distance, away from Loeb, as he considered the possibilities. With sudden realization, Gordon spun around. "Wait!"

But, Loeb was already choking. He stumbled back, grasping at his throat, gasping for air. The tumbler fell out of his hand, shattering against the hard desk. Whiskey spilled across the smooth redwood and within seconds the liquid was smoking, eating its way through the wood, biting into the metal beneath.

"Get a medic!" Gordon shouted, even though he knew it was too late.

Chapter Eleven

While Detective Wuertz scoured the city to find Harvey Dent, the Joker's third target, Dent was arriving at the fundraising party that Bruce Wayne was hosting in his honour.

Even though Rachel knew Harvey was uncomfortable in this wealthy crowd, she encouraged him to mingle. Leaving him to work the crowd on his own, Rachel walked off to say 'hello' to a woman she knew.

Alfred approached with a drink. "A little liquid courage, Mr. Dent?"

"Thanks." Dent recognized Alfred as Bruce Wayne's butler and, knowing Rachel grew up at Wayne Manor, asked, "You've known Rachel her whole life?"

"Not yet, sir," Alfred replied with dry humour.

Dent smiled, surveying the people socializing in the elegant room. "Any psychotic ex-boyfriends I should be aware of?" he asked playfully.

Alfred shook his head at the question. "Oh, you have *no* idea..."

Dent was puzzled by Alfred's reply, but didn't have a chance to delve into its hidden meaning. The pulsating whirr of helicopter blades overcame the soft music and conversation in the room, which halted under the deafening roar.

Bruce Wayne's private helicopter was touching down outside on his helipad. The door of the chopper opened and Bruce, dressed to the nines in a designer tuxedo, stepped out gracefully, a clutch of supermodels surrounding him.

Once the helicopter flew off, Bruce used his dramatic entrance to hold everyone's attention.

"Sorry, I'm late," he told his friends. "I'm so glad you started without me!" Bruce's eyes darted around the room. "Where's Rachel?"

Rachel cringed at her name being called, but Wayne spotted her and drew her up through the crowd to where he was standing in the centre of the room.

"When Rachel told me she was dating Harvey Dent, I had one thing to say." He paused for effect. "The guy from those awful campaign commercials?"

Laughter echoed through the penthouse. Harvey Dent shifted his weight between his feet and looked away in a feeble attempt to mask his embarrassment.

"I believe in Harvey Dent." Bruce held up a copy of Dent's campaign poster. It was striped in red, white, and blue. An American flag waved down the centre, overlaid with a picture of Harvey Dent and the very words that Bruce had just spoken.

"Nice slogan, Harvey," Bruce said, putting the poster down. "Certainly caught Rachel's attention." Next to Bruce, Rachel blushed even more crimson. "But then I started paying attention to Harvey, too, and kept my eye on the things he's been doing as our new D.A., and you know what?" Bruce pointed a finger at himself. "Now, *I* believe in Harvey Dent." A cheer rose from the crowd.

Bruce rode the wave of applause and continued, "On his watch, Gotham feels a little safer. A little more optimistic. So," he told his friends, "get out your chequebooks and let's make sure that he stays right where all of Gotham wants him!" Alfred passed Bruce a glass of champagne, which he raised high in a toast. "To the face of Gotham's bright future – Harvey Dent."

With a gracious nod to Bruce, Dent smiled, accepting the toast.

A short while later, while Harvey worked the crowd, collecting donation checks, Rachel found Bruce standing on the penthouse balcony, contemplating Gotham.

"Harvey may not know you well enough to understand when you're making fun of him. But I do," Rachel reprimanded Bruce.

Bruce shook his head. "I meant every word," he assured her, moving closer and taking her arm.

"Rachel," he breathed, struggling to tell her how he felt. "The day you once told me about, the day when Gotham no longer needs Batman, it's coming."

Rachel's mind flashed back to that day, not so long ago, when they stood together in the charred remains of Wayne Manor. They'd kissed, and then she had told Bruce that they could not be together as long as he was Batman. They both had known it was impossible. Gotham needed Batman and he could not give up the role until someone else came along to be Gotham's hero, so they'd parted, remaining friends.

"It's happening now," Brue said excitedly. "Harvey is the hero. He locked up half the city's criminals, and he did it without wearing a mask. Gotham needs a champion with a face."

"You can't ask me to wait for that-" Rachel began. A noise at the balcony door made her stop and turn. It was Harvey

Dent.

Unaware of what he was interrupting, Dent came out onto the balcony, casually saying, "You sure can throw a party, Wayne. Thanks again." He shook Bruce's hand vigorously. "Mind if I borrow Rachel?"

Rachel glanced over her shoulder at Bruce as Dent wrapped his arm around her to lead her back into the bustle of the party.

Hopeful that she'd someday be his, Bruce stared after the two of them for a few moments before re-entering the party himself.

Keeping his arm tight around Rachel, Dent led her past his new supporters into the kitchen. He closed the door solidly behind them.

Dent was visibly more at ease in the silence of the empty kitchen than he was in the commotion of the packed living room "You cannot leave me alone with these people," he said, his tension rapidly dissipating.

Rachel didn't understand. "The whole mob is after you and you're worried about these guys?"

Dent sighed. "Compared to this, the mob doesn't scare me." He thought about it a moment, then added, "Although, I will say that having them gunning for you makes you see things clearly." He paused before continuing. "Facing death makes you think about what you couldn't stand losing. And who you want to spend the rest of you life with." He ended his sentence with a big smile at Rachel.

"The rest of your life, huh?" Rachel's heart was speeding up. She hadn't expected to have this conversation with Harvey.

Not tonight. "That's a pretty big commitment."

Dent laughed. He knew that the rest of his life might be years or minutes. It all depended on if they could keep the members of the mob behind bars. "What's your answer?" Dent asked without preamble.

Could she marry Harvey Dent, Rachel wondered. She wasn't sure yet. "I don't have an answer," she replied.

"It's someone else, isn't it?" Dent pressed, needing to know what was holding her back.

But Rachel was having trouble focusing on what Dent was saying. She was distracted by Bruce Wayne, who had snuck into the kitchen, coming up fast behind Dent.

"Just tell me it's not Wayne," Dent told Rachel. "The guy's a complete-"

Rachel's eyes opened wide and she gasped as Bruce grabbed Dent in a sleeper hold from behind. Dent slumped against Bruce.

"What are you doing?!" Rachel angrily demanded, shocked at Bruce's actions against Harvey.

"They've come for him." Bruce quickly filled her in. "I just got a call. The Joker's men have killed Judge Surrillo and Commissioner Loeb."

Rachel couldn't believe it and was about to accuse Bruce of making up the story, when gunshots rang out from the living room. Guests at the party began to scream.

Bruce told Rachel that he had gone back onto the balcony for a breath of fresh air when the doorbell rang. It was Detective Wuertz. Alfred let him in, not realizing that behind Wuertz, with a gun to his head, was the Joker.

The Joker was currently in the living room, searching for

Harvey Dent.

Another gunshot echoed through the apartment penthouse and Rachel jumped. She didn't stop Bruce from stuffing Dent into a closet. In fact, Rachel handed him the handle of a broom to use as a temporary lock.

"Stay hidden," Bruce warned her as he slipped through the kitchen door, into the pandemonium.

In the master bedroom, behind a false wall, Bruce Wayne entered a secret room. Not a minute later, Batman emerged, waiting for the perfect time to attack.

The Joker was moving through the party, his fake smile striking horror in the hearts of all the guests.

"I only have one question," he told a woman who was quivering and clinging to her husband. "Where is Harvey Dent?" The woman couldn't answer. No one could. "Fine," the Joker announced, "Then I'll settle for his loved ones…"

A distinguished gentleman stepped into the Joker's path. "We're not intimidated by thugs."

The Joker smiled at the man. "You know, you remind me of my father." Joker, quick as lightening, grabbed the man. "I hated my father." He shoved the man to the side.

Rachel could not remain silently hidden, it went against who she was inside and out. "Stop!" she shouted, stepping boldly into the room.

The Joker turned to Rachel. His grin seemed to widen into an even larger, more grotesque smile. "Hello, beautiful," he said, grabbing her arm and pulling her close, holding a knife to her face. He touched Rachel's cheek with the flat part of his knife. "You must be Harvey's squeeze. You look nervous. It's the scars, isn't it?"

Rachel didn't respond. She kept her gaze steady and refused to show him fear.

"Wanna know how I got them?" the Joker asked. "I had a wife, beautiful like you. Who told me I worry too much. Who said I need to smile more. Who gambled. And got in deep with the sharks. One day they beat her up and make a mess of her face." He paused, pressing the cold blade of his knife tighter against Rachel's cheek. "I loved her so much, I cut my own face to match. Fickle woman, she didn't like my new look, so she left me."

The Joker was so close now, Rachel could smell his stale breath. "Now I'm always smiling." He paused, squinting, considering, then said, "Or maybe I got my smile when my father cut me up with a knife. He thought I was too serious a kid, so he wanted to 'put a smile on my face.'" He laughed hysterically at his own stories. Truth was not part of his game.

Stepping back slightly, he removed the knife from Rachel's cheek. She took advantage of the distance and balled her fist, slugging him hard in the face.

The Joker touched the sore spot on his cheek and mocked, "A little fight in you. I like that."

From out of nowhere, a booming voice responded. "Then you're going to love me!"

Batman pounced, catching the Joker with a powerful blow, and the clown stumbled back, giving Batman the opening he needed to grab the knife.

The Joker had not come to the party alone. Thugs accompanied him and Batman fought hard to take them out, two at a time. He'd nearly accomplished his task, ready to return to his ultimate battle with the mastermind of evil, the Joker, when the Joker kicked at him with a knife that protruded from his shoe. The knife caught Batman between the armored plates of his Batsuit, right in the vulnerable spot Lucius had warned about.

Ignoring his own blood and pain, Batman crouched, then leapt toward the Joker, grabbing him around the waist and hurling him across the room. "Drop the knife," Batman commanded.

"Sure," the Joker replied, making no move to follow the order. "Just take off your mask and show us who you are."

Rachel shook her head 'no' at Batman.

"Fine then," the Joker said, raising the stakes. He pulled out a shotgun and blasted a pane of glass in the window next to him. Dragging Rachel over to the hole, Joker then dangled Rachel by one arm out the window.

"Let her go," Batman's voice was steady and serious.

"Very poor choice of words," The Joker laughed and opened his fist.

Rachel was falling. No one could survive the drop from Wayne's penthouse, atop one of Gotham's highest buildings, to the pavement below. As she rolled down a sloping glass roof, sliding toward the edge, Batman dove for her, but missed on his first attempt. She was falling too fast.

SWOOSH! Batman fired his grapple, snagging Rachel's ankle. Activating the fabric of his cape, he managed to slow their descent, but not enough to prevent a crash.

SLAM! Batman enveloped Rachel in his cape as together they smashed into the hood of a taxi.

The driver screamed as they rolled off the hood of his car, down the windshield and onto the pavement. They were scraped and bruised, but thankfully alive.

The Joker had followed Batman down to the street, hoping to witness a major splat on the sidewalk. But this show was better than the one he'd planned. He was breathing heavily, exhilarated by the action scene that had unfolded.

Joker got into his waiting car. "What about Dent?" the driver asked.

"I'm a man of my word," the Joker replied, not worried that he hadn't accomplished his goal yet, as his car pulled out and zoomed away.

When Harvey Dent was released from Bruce's kitchen, he was determined not to let the Joker's threats keep him from his task of cleaning up Gotham. He rushed out of the penthouse, bound for the MCU, where he planned to interview Lau himself and hopefully discover, once and for all, the identity of the man behind the circus mask.

Chapter Twelve

Early the next morning, Alfred descended the rickety elevator again to discover Bruce Wayne in the Bat-Bunker, surrounded by video screens all showing different images of the Joker.

By the expression on his face, Alfred knew that Bruce was deeply troubled not only by the deaths of Judge Surrillo and Commissioner Loeb, but that the Joker had linked Batman to the murders by demanding he reveal himself.

"Targeting me won't get their money back," Bruce said, with a long sigh. "I knew the mob wouldn't go down without a fight, but this is different. By linking themselves to the Joker, they've crossed a line."

"You crossed it first, sir," Alfred pointed out in a fatherly tone. "You've hammered them, squeezed them to the point of desperation. And now, in their desperation they've turned to a man they don't fully understand." Alfred walked across the room, opening a cabinet to reveal the Batsuit gleaming under a single light bulb.

Bruce looked at the suit, considering. "Criminals aren't complicated, Alfred. We just have to figure out what this Joker person is after."

Alfred shook his head. "Respectfully, Master Wayne, perhaps this is a man you don't fully understand."

Bruce agreed that he was having trouble figuring out what it was that the Joker wanted, but disagreed that criminals could be complicated. He repeated to Alfred that he simply needed to figure out what the Joker was after.

Alfred disagreed again, then told Bruce a story to support his claim:

"When I was in Burma, a long time ago, my friends and I were working for the local government, which was trying to buy the loyalty of tribal leaders by bribing them with precious stones. However, their caravans carrying the precious stones were being raided by a bandit who was stealing the jewels. The tribal leaders asked us if we could take care of the problem. So we started looking for the stones to track him down. But after six months, we still couldn't find anyone who traded with him."

After listening carefully, Bruce asked, "What were you missing?"

"One day I saw a child playing with a ruby the size of a tangerine." Alfred shrugged. "The bandit had been throwing away the stones after he stole them."

Bruce was puzzled. "Why was he stealing them?"

Alfred answered, "Because he thought it was good sport. Because some men aren't looking for anything logical, like money. They can't be bought, bullied, reasoned, or negotiated with." Alfred's voice dropped to a whisper which still echoed through the concrete bunker. "Some men just want to watch the world burn."

On a rooftop overlooking Gotham, Batman crouched, using his newest piece of technology to listen to a million voices. Could Alfred be right? Could the Joker's antics be just for the fun of causing death, destruction, and chaos with no greater purpose?

Batman considered the possibility as he tapped his earpiece. Even with all the chatter, it was surprisingly easy to distinguish between normal conversations about dinner plans and TV shows from the specific voices he was targeting. Now all he needed to do was connect Fox's sonar mapping devise to his transmitter and he'd be able to hear the Joker and pinpoint his location. The Joker's games had to come to an end.

After a while, with no sign of the Joker, Batman decided to quit for the night. He had begun to take out his earpiece, ready to move on, when two voices caught his attention. One man was telling another that they had found Harvey Dent dead, in an apartment at 8th Street and Orchard Avenue.

Shocked, since he thought Dent was safe, Batman hurried to the address.

When he arrived, Lieutenant Gordon and Detective Ramirez were about to crash down the apartment door, guns drawn. BAM! Gordon slammed open the door, then cautiously entered, pointing his gun steadily at the silence of the room.

Gordon moved carefully though the apartment, searching for Dent. There!

At the kitchen table sat, propped up like rag dolls, were two dead men. They were holding cards as if enjoying a game of poker. Gordon glanced at the playing cards in their hands and reported that they were all jokers. Crude leers were carved into the men's faces and their driver's licenses were pinned to their chests.

Gordon leaned in closer. One man was Patrick Harvey. The other, Richard Dent.

"Harvey… Dent," Gordon shook his head at the irony of the Joker's deadly prank.

Batman stepped from the shadows onto the scene.

Detective Ramirez immediately turned on him, pointing at the two innocent men at the table. "It's because of you that these guys are dead in the first place!" Obviously, she'd seen the Joker's threat on television.

Gordon gave Ramirez a firm look and she backed off, but Batman had received her message loud and clear.

Batman scanned the room until he found what he was looking for: A bullet in the wall. Using a blade from his utility belt, Batman didn't cut out the bullet but instead removed the entire brick.

When Gordon questioned him, Batman told the Lieutenant that he was going to look for fingerprints on the bullet.

Gordon didn't stop Batman. He could have told him that it was a police investigation and to hand over the brick, but instead Gordon replied, "Whatever you're gonna do, do it fast, because we know his next target-"

Lieutenant Gordon directed Batman's attention to a poster on the apartment wall. Re-elect Mayor Garcia.

The photo of the Mayor had been transformed - his smile had been redrawn in red crayon into a maniacal clown's grin. And underneath the photo, in messy scrawled writing, it said "Ha Ha Ha."

Lucius Fox was sitting at his desk at Wayne Enterprises trying to catch up on some paperwork when Reese, the consultant lawyer, walked in with an unusually smug grin on his face.

Lucius looked up from his papers. "What can I do for you, Mr. Reese?"

Reese told him that he'd stayed late at work to review the numbers on L.S.I. Holdings. "I found irregularities," Reese reported.

Fox gave Reese a questioning look. He should have ended the review days ago after Fox returned from Hong Kong, when the business arrangement had been cancelled.

"Their CEO is in police custody," Fox replied with a wave of his hand, indicating that Reese should have long ago moved on to another project.

But Reese would not be easily dismissed. "The problem," he informed Fox, "was not with their numbers, but with yours." He shot Fox a sideways look. "A whole division of Wayne Enterprises disappeared overnight, so I went down to the archives and started pulling old files." From his briefcase, Reese pulled out a wrinkled, smudged, folded blueprint and slid it across the desk. He grinned. "My kids love the Batman. I thought he was pretty cool. Out there, kicking some ass." He paused while Fox opened the blueprint. It was a drawing he'd made during his days down in R and D. An old image of the Tumbler, now known citywide as the Batmobile.

"Changes things when you know it's just a rich kid playing dress up," Reese said with a smarmy chuckle. Reese leaned over Fox's shoulder to point out the place where Fox had signed off on the drawing in the corner. "What are you building him now? A rocket ship?" Reese laughed at his own bad joke, then stood up straight and made his demand. "I want ten million a year. For the rest of my life."

Fox looked at him, his face full of wonder. "Let me get this straight. You think that your client, one of the wealthiest and most powerful men in the world, is secretly a vigilante who spends his nights beating criminals to a pulp with his bare hands?" He paused just long enough to fold up the blueprint. "And now your plan is to blackmail him?"

Fox slid the blueprint across his desk, back to the still grinning Reese.

"Well, then," Fox said with a curt nod. "Good luck."

Reese's face dropped, clearly disappointed that things had not gone as he planned. Leaving the blueprint on the table, he walked solemnly out of Lucius Fox's office.

As Reese descended in one elevator bank, Bruce Wayne ascended in another. He'd brought the bullet from the "Harvey and Dent" murder scene to Lucius for analysis.

Fox and Bruce went down to Applied Sciences together.

Fox scanned the bullet and within minutes had discovered a thumbprint. He couldn't identify it, but he was more than willing to make copies.

While Bruce waited, Fox turned from his computer desk and asked, "Mr. Wayne, did you reassign R and D?"

"Yes." Bruce confirmed what Mr. Reese had discovered about the allocation of funds at Wayne Enterprises. Fox asked for more information, but Bruce would only tell him that he was working on 'a new government telecommunications project.'

Fox handed Bruce the image of the thumbprint off the computer printer. "I wasn't aware we had any new government contracts. Can you-"

Bruce squinted his eyes as a subtle caution to Lucius to ask no more questions. "I'm playing this one pretty close to the chest," he said.

Lucius got the message. "Fair enough." But he couldn't help looking at Bruce uneasily as he left the lab.

An exact match couldn't be found. As hard as he tried, Bruce couldn't figure out whose print was on that bullet.

"I ran it through all the databases and came up with four possibilities," he told Alfred, moving away from the computer bank to let Alfred take his chair. Bruce was in a hurry so his time was at a premium. Alfred took over the work at the computer.

While Alfred searched for a match, Bruce rolled out his newest purchase - a gleaming, top-of-the-line, motorcycle. He moved the bike into the elevator with the understanding that Alfred would contact him as soon as he found a match.

As the elevator doors began to close, Alfred announced with his usual calmness, "Got one."

Bruce slammed his hand into the crack between the closing doors, forcing the elevator to reopen. He looked out at Alfred.

"Melvin White. Aggravated assault. Moved to Arkham twice. 1502 Randolf Apartments, just off State-"

He didn't wait for the rest. Letting the elevator doors creak shut, Bruce Wayne knew exactly where he was headed.

Chapter Thirteen

The funeral parade for Gotham's fallen Commissioner was filled with pomp and circumstance. Uniformed officers were marching in rows following the coffin, draped with an American flag, toward a dais where Rachel and Harvey sat with the Mayor and Lieutenant Gordon.

The street at Parkside Avenue was blocked off. Onlookers lined the sidewalks. It seemed that most of Gotham City had turned out to say goodbye to Commissioner Loeb.

Bruce Wayne skirted traffic on his cycle as he surveyed the scene, storing details in his mind.

Mike Engel, the TV reporter, was there. Bruce could hear him say into a live camera, "With no word from the Batman even as they mourn Commissioner Loeb, these cops have to be wondering if the Joker is going to make good on his threat to kill the Mayor today."

Bruce scanned the buildings, noting the police snipers on practically every rooftop.

1502. He found the Randolf Apartments, an old and grungy building near the funeral site. The tenants eyed him warily as Bruce dismounted his motorcycle and hurried up the stairs. He could hear the Mayor at the microphone below, beginning the service.

The door shattered on its hinges when Bruce kicked it in. Inside the dingy apartment, eight men, wearing nothing but their underwear, were bound, gagged, and blindfolded. A man yelped in pain as Bruce ripped the tape from his mouth.

"They took," he was breathing hard, fighting to get the words out, "...they took our guns, our uniforms..." Bruce realized that these were the SWAT team members, sent to the apartment building towering over where the Mayor was now addressing the assembled mourners, to protect the Mayor.

Knowing trouble was on its way, Bruce ran to the window just as Mayor Garcia was closing his remarks. It was too late for action. Bruce could only watch in horror as what appeared to be the honour guard, meant to be firing a salute to the late Commissioner, stepped forward and raised their weapons. Not into the air to fire blanks, but tragically pointing straight at the Mayor.

Even from where he stood, Bruce could see one of the honour guard's faces. He'd recognize that gruesome grim anywhere. The Joker.

The honour guard fired at the Mayor, who didn't have time to duck. Lieutenant Gordon, acting solely on instinct, dove in front of him, pushing him to the ground and, at the same time, taking a bullet himself.

Bruce could no longer tell what was happening. The crowd was screaming, people running, and his last view was of the Joker and his 'honour guard' disappearing into the crush.

Harvey Dent managed to pull himself away from the commotion. He'd seen one of the Joker's men go down, shot in the leg by a SWAT sniper. Dent knew the man was now in the back of an ambulance, but there was no way Dent was going to give up this opportunity and let him go directly to the hospital. There were some things Dent needed to know first.

Distracting the ambulance driver, Dent leapt into the front seat and drove the Joker's man away to a private location.

A little while later, across town, Detective Stephens and another uniformed officer from MCU solemnly knocked on Barbara Gordon's door. Stephens had been given the horrible job of telling the Lieutenant's wife that her husband has been killed.

Barbara stared up at the cop in disbelief, and told her young son, James, to take his sister into the other room. Then something outside the front door caught her attention.

"Are you out there?" she shouted into the black night. "Are you?"

Little James Gordon had not done as his mother commanded. He was standing at her feet, pointing at the man perched in the shadows. Batman.

Barbara couldn't control her sorrow or her anger. "You brought this on us! This craziness! You did! You brought this…" Her voice broke off as Barbara collapsed into Detective Stephens' arms.

Dent drove the Joker's thug to the basement of an abandoned apartment building. It took a few minutes of questioning, but he had his answer. He knew who the Joker's next target was. He picked up his phone to warn Rachel Dawes.

In the chaotic halls of MCU, with cops and eyewitnesses crammed in every available chair and interview space, Rachel Dawes answered her phone.

"Harvey Dent, where are you?!" Rachel wanted to know.

Dent didn't answer the question, choosing to ask instead, "Where are you?"

He could hear Rachel's annoyance when she replied, "I'm where you should be – at Major Crimes trying to sort through all the-"

He cut her off. "Rachel, listen to me, you're not safe there."

She didn't understand his urgency. "This is Gordon's unit, Harvey."

"Gordon's gone, Rachel." Dent's voice was laced with anger.

"He vouched for these men-" Rachel insisted.

"…and he's gone," Dent interjected. "I just heard that the Joker's named you next."

There was a pause on Rachel's side. She didn't respond, so Dent continued, "Rachel, I can't let anything happen to you. I love you too much. Is there someone, anyone in the city we can trust?"

Rachel didn't miss a beat. "Bruce. We can trust Bruce Wayne."

Dent wasn't so sure. "Rachel, I know he's your friend, but-"

"Trust me, Harvey." Even though she was now whispering, Rachel's voice was strong and certain. "Bruce's penthouse is now the safest place in the city."

Dent relented. "Okay. Go straight there. Don't tell anyone where you're going. I'll find you there." And then, after she hung up, Dent added in a low voice, "I love you."

Switching easily from protecting his girlfriend to

investigating a crime, Dent hung up the phone and glared at the blindfolded man tied to a chair in front of him.

Kidnapping and violence wasn't Dent's usual fare, but with Rachel's life in the balance, it was rapidly becoming a large part of who he was.

Dent ripped off the man's blindfold and showed him a loaded gun. He waved the gun in the thug's face and asked for information about how to find and stop the Joker, but the man gave nothing.

"Do you wanna play games?" Dent demanded, shoving the barrel of his gun against the man's temple. With his other hand, he pulled out his lucky coin. "Heads, you get to keep your head. Tails, not so lucky. So," he gave the man one last chance, "do you want to tell me about the Joker?"

When the thug didn't reply, Dent sent the coin soaring with a flick of his wrist. It landed and Dent pressed the coin against his gun hand. "Heads." The thug exhaled, relieved for the moment.

But Dent didn't stop there. "Go again?" he asked.

The Joker's thug began to sob. "I don't know anything."

Dent shrugged. He'd play all day until the man gave him what he wanted. "You're not playing the odds, friend." He flipped his coin up for a second toss.

The coin never landed.

"You'd leave a man's life to chance?" Batman looked down at the coin in his gloved hand.

"Not exactly," Dent answered, holding out his hand for his silver dollar.

"What do you expect to learn from him?" Batman asked, indicating that the man was clearly a nutjob, simply hired for a fee to do the Joker's bidding.

Dent knocked over a chair in frustration. "The Joker killed Gordon and Loeb and now, he's going to kill Rachel!" Dent would do anything to keep that from happening.

Batman gave Dent a minute to calm himself, then said, "You're the symbol of hope that I could never be. Your stand against organized crime is the first legitimate ray of light in Gotham for decades. If anyone saw this," he indicated the thug bound to the chair, cowering in fear, "everything would be undone – all the criminals you got off the streets would be released. And Jim Gordon would have died for nothing." Batman placed the coin back in Dent's hand.

"You're going to call a press conference," Batman instructed. "Tomorrow morning."

"Why?" Dent asked. He had a sneaking suspicion that Batman was about to play into the Joker's demands. And he was right.

"No one else will die because of me," Batman told Dent with a tone of finality. "Gotham is in your hands now."

"You can't! You can't give in!" Dent shouted, but his words merely echoed off the walls in the abandoned basement. Once again, Batman had disappeared like a shadow in the night.

Rachel found a safe refuge in Bruce Wayne's penthouse. With Alfred to cater to her needs, and Bruce to protect her, she felt certain that the Joker couldn't touch her.

After a brief conversation on her phone, Rachel went out onto the balcony to find Bruce. He was, as always, standing at the rail, overlooking the city. His city.

"Harvey just called," she told Bruce, plopping down into the empty chair next to where Bruce stood. "He says Batman is going to turn himself in."

Bruce moved from the rail and sat in the chair next to Rachel. "I have no choice," he sighed, leaning back into the chair and closing his eyes.

"You honestly think it's going to stop the Joker from killing?" Rachel stared at him as if he'd lost his mind.

Bruce opened his eyes to look at her. "Perhaps not, but I've got enough blood on my hands." He glanced down at his hands, clenched into a fighter's fists. "I've seen, now, what I would have to become to stop men like him." Bruce stood and moved back over by the railing.

By the expression on her friend's face, Rachel knew his decision was final. She got up and followed him over to the rails, standing nearby, but not too close.

Bruce turned to face her. "You once told me that if the day came when I was finished-" he took a step closer to Rachel, "we'd be together."

Rachel stayed planted where she was. Not moving in toward him, or away. "Bruce, don't make me your one hope for a normal life."

In a sudden sweep, he pulled her into his arms.

"Did you mean it?" he asked very simply.

"Yes," Rachel replied, but then pulled slightly back. "But they won't let us be together after you turn yourself in."

They couldn't be together if he continued being Batman and couldn't be together if he gave it up. Bruce understood the conundrum and left the balcony without glancing back.

Rachel felt sad as she watched him leave. He would survive

without her. And she would have to move forward. Harvey Dent was waiting for her answer to his marriage proposal. Now, she was ready to give him one.

While Bruce drove off into the night, Rachel sat down to write him a letter.

In the Bat-Bunker, Alfred and Bruce were busy erasing all ties either of them had to Batman. By dawn, they had burned almost everything: documents, blueprints, designs, and files. Even the logs that Alfred had fastidiously kept, chronicling Batman's adventures.

"Burn anything that could lead back to Lucius or Rachel," Bruce told Alfred, handing him another pile of loose papers.

Alfred took the documents and placed them in the incinerator, but shook his head while he did it.

Bruce knew that Alfred didn't approve of his plan to turn himself in, but Bruce felt that he had no choice. The Joker had taken away his right to exist. "People are dying," Bruce told him. "What would you have me do?"

Alfred stopped shovelling materials into the blazing fire. He stared deeply into Bruce's eyes with a fearsome gaze.

"Endure, Master Wayne," Alfred told him, hands firmly on his hips. "Take it. They'll hate you for it, but that's the point of Batman…he can be the outcast. He can make the choice no one else can face. The right choice."

"No." Bruce shook his head vehemently. "Today I found out what Batman can't do. He can't endure this." With a shrug and a rueful smile, Bruce sighed. "Today, you get to say, 'I told you so.'"

"Today, I don't want to," Alfred said, watching Bruce closet the Batsuit for the final time. Alfred turned off the lights, powering down the bunker, and they headed to the elevator. With one last, winsome look back, Alfred couldn't help but add, "Although I did bloody tell you." Alfred pressed the button to call the lift. "I suppose they'll lock me up as well. Your accomplice."

Bruce laughed. His voice was rich and deep in the darkened space. "Accomplice?" he gave another throaty laugh. "I'm going to tell them the whole thing was your idea."

Chapter Fourteen

"Ladies and Gentlemen," Harvey Dent began the press conference. He looked out at the full-to-capacity crowd, noting the presence of Bruce Wayne in back of the room. Dent was glad that Wayne had come to witness the press conference. He appreciated his support.

"Thank you for coming. I've called this press conference for two reasons. Firstly, to assure the citizens of Gotham that everything that can be done over the Joker killings is being done. The killings will now come to an end, because Batman has offered to turn himself in."

A boisterous cheer rose from the crowd.

"So where is he?" a heckler called out.

Dent kept his cool. "First, let us consider the situation: should we give in to this terrorist's demands? Do we really think that-"

A reporter shouted out from the back of the room, "You'd rather protect an outlaw vigilante than the lives of citizens?"

The crowd erupted, everyone talking at once.

With a wave of his hands, Dent motioned the noisy crowd to settle down.

"Batman is an outlaw," he agreed. "But that's not why we're demanding he turn himself in. We're doing it because we're scared. We've been happy to let Batman clean up our streets for us until now."

The heckler interrupted again. "Things are worse than ever." There were murmurs of agreement.

Dent surveyed the angry crowd. When he was ready to speak again, he tilted the microphone closer to his mouth and leaned in, impassioned.

"Yes. They are, but *the night is darkest just before the dawn*. And I promise you, the dawn is coming." At that, the crowd settled into an uneasy silence. "One day the Batman will have to answer for the laws he's broken – but to us, not this madman."

It was rapidly becoming apparent that Dent was not going to reveal Batman to the crowd and they were becoming more restless. A chant broke out, "No more dead cops! No more dead cops!"

The reporter pushed her way to the front of the room, demanding to know, "Where is the Batman?"

As the crowd continued to chant, Dent knew that he had lost the battle. The citizens of Gotham were more concerned with arresting Batman than they were with standing up to the Joker.

Dent noticed Bruce Wayne begin to stand. Even though he was unclear why Wayne would be rising at that moment, Dent didn't really care. He had a plan of action and it was time to implement it.

"So be it!" Dent shouted above the crowd. He turned to the

officers, "Take the Batman into custody." The room fell silent. And in that space, Dent offered up his own wrists to the officers. "I am the Batman."

Cuffed, head held high, Harvey Dent allowed himself to be ushered out of the chaotic press room, right past Bruce Wayne, who was staring at him, mouth open, jaw slack, full of surprise.

Rachel could not believe what she was seeing! Harvey Dent was being arrested for claiming to be Batman. She knew it wasn't true. She spun around to Alfred, who was standing behind her, watching the television over her shoulder.

"Why is he letting Harvey do this, Alfred?" she asked, completely appalled.

Alfred put a comforting arm across her shoulder. "Perhaps both Bruce and Mr. Dent believe that Batman stands for more than a terrorist's whims, Ms. Dawes, even if everyone hates him for it. That's the sacrifice he's making – to not be a hero. To be something more."

Rachel pulled away, rejecting Alfred's reassurance. She was angry and began to pace across the floor. "Well, you're right about one thing – letting Harvey take the fall is not heroic." She reached into her purse and brought out an envelope. Rachel handed it to Alfred. "You know Bruce best," she said, handing Alfred the letter she had written a short while ago. "Give it to him when the time is right."

Rachel slipped into her coat. She was not going to remain hidden while Harvey went to jail.

Alfred held the letter gingerly, understanding instinctively that Rachel had poured her heart into the envelope. "How will I know when?" he asked.

"It's not sealed," Rachel said. Then, she leaned in and gave him a kiss on the cheek. "Goodbye, Alfred."

Alfred walked her to the door, knowing he could not hold her in the penthouse any longer. She wouldn't have stayed even if he'd begged her to.

"Goodbye, Rachel." Alfred closed the door gently behind her.

Rachel arrived at MCU just as Harvey was being shuttled into a waiting armoured police van.

Dent smiled as Rachel approached, and the escorting officers allowed the two of them to have a moment together.

"I'm sorry. I didn't have time to talk this through with you," Harvey said, looking at Rachel's eyes searchingly.

On her way over Rachel had realized what Harvey's full plan was. He was anticipating that the Joker would make an attempt to get to him while the police transferred him to Central Holding He was ready and, he hoped, so was Batman.

"This is the Joker's chance, and when he attacks, Batman will take him down," Harvey explained.

"Don't offer yourself as bait, Harvey," Rachel pleaded. "This is too dangerous."

Dent grinned and, looping his cuffed hands around her neck, pulled her in for a kiss. "I have an idea," he said. Then, pulling back his hands and bending slightly, he reached down into his pocket. Dent pulled out his lucky dollar. "Heads I go through with it."

"This is your life," Rachel chastised him. "You don't leave something like this to chance."

"I'm not." Dent tossed the coin to Rachel. She caught it and opened her hand. It was heads. He was going through with his plan. As the doors closed to the van and it slipped into place in a long line of police car escorts, Rachel turned the coin over in her hand.

Heads on both sides.

She thought about all the other times he'd pretended to determine fate on a coin toss. It wasn't fate at all. Rachel watched the convoy pull away. "You make your own luck," she said to no one but herself.

Chapter Fifteen

The armoured vehicle with Dent inside moved swiftly through Gotham's streets. The commanding officer had instructed the driver not to stop for any reason, so the driver was a bit shaken when he noticed a burning fire truck in the middle of the street ahead, causing traffic to stand still. He pressed on the van's breaks and prepared to break orders. He was going to have to stop.

In the rear of the van, Dent sat with a team of SWAT in full protective gear, including bulletproof vests and helmets. Dent was patiently awaiting the Joker's attack. Expecting it. And when he felt the van began to slow, he knew it was coming soon.

They were changing route. The driver of the van calmly took the radio and announced to the rest of the convoy, "All units be advised... All units will exit down Cheviot West and proceed north on Lower 5th Avenue."

The SWAT sitting next to the driver couldn't believe what he'd heard. "Lower 5th?" he exclaimed. "We'll be like ducks in a barrel down there."

But there was no other choice. The road was blocked ahead and they had precious cargo to deliver to Central Holding. The van made a sharp turn down the nearest exit and onto the subterranean streets.

Down on Lower 5th, a garbage truck broke into the convoy by swiping a number of police cars off the road. Moving swiftly into position behind the armoured van, the garbage truck shortened the gap, barrelling ahead until it slammed into the van's bumper.

Inside, Harvey Dent was smiling. The time had come.

"Get us out of here," the SWAT team member in the passenger seat shouted to the driver. The driver nailed the gas, but the garbage truck was hot on its heels, pushing the van forward, bumper to bumper. The SWAT team member grabbed the radio, calling for backup support. "We've got company back here," he announced, yelling into the receiver.

He hadn't put the radio away when SLAM! A second truck smashed into the front of the armoured car. A label on the truck's side clearly used to read LAUGHTER, but someone had added an S in front of the original word, making it SLAUGHTER.

That someone was the Joker, who was hanging out the back as he fired shots at the armoured van, laughing all the while.

Hearing the shots all around, Harvey Dent continued to grin, calmly enjoying the battle he had predicted.

The Joker changed weapons. A rocket launcher was now aimed at the white van. Seeing that massive weapon pointed right at them, the driver of the armoured van attempted to dodge left, then right, crashing past parked cars and swerving into traffic. But with the Joker's truck in front and the garbage truck still behind him, escape seemed impossible.

BLAM! The Joker shot his weapon, but missed. He hit a nearby police car. It exploded in a fireball.

And through that humongous fireball, a dark form suddenly appeared. It crashed through the blast with a blast of its own.

As Dent had predicted, Batman had arrived.

The Batmobile was coming to the armoured van's aid, slamming through traffic, stopping for no one. Batman was still a few rows of parked cars away when he noticed that the Joker was reloading, preparing to take out the van in a fiery burst.

Batman toggled the afterburner and the Batmobile rocketed over the other cars. The Joker turned, quickly taking aim at Batman, instead of the van, and fired.

A direct hit. The rear of the Batmobile exploded on impact, bursting into flames and spinning out of control.

The Joker was thrilled. His cackling laughter reverberated through the darkened streets.

The Batmobile flipped over and over, finally coming to rest in a smouldering heap.

The front was intact, but the rear wheels were scattered across the roadway. A small crowd came to see what had happened not just to the car, but to the driver as well.

A boy peered into the wreckage of the Batmobile. "He isn't here," the boy announced to the crowd, brimming with anticipation. "He's gone."

The crowd was watching the Batmobile, searching for any signs of Batman's whereabouts, when suddenly, the front of the car began to shift. One front wheel pushed up, bringing the other wheel alongside, forming a high-tech motorcycle. Seated on this motorcycle, this Bat-Pod, hunched low over the controls, was Batman.

From the wreckage of the Batmobile, the Bat-Pod shot forward, bursting free as the Batmobile self-destructed, totally consumed in a massive fireball. Batman's cape sucked together forming a tight pack on his shoulders as he cleared the churning wreckage of the Batmobile and set off after the armuored van and the SLAUGHTER truck.

Batman pursued the truck, tearing off the side mirrors from parked cars as he passed. He was roaring down the street, blasting his way closer to the Joker's truck.

When he reached striking distance, Batman fired a harpoon at the truck. It caught its mark, just below the bumper. Batman zoomed ahead, wrapping the cables attached to the harpoon around a lamp post, and only then did he stop, grinding to a halt. There, by the streetlamp, Batman waited, watching to see what would happen.

The Joker's truck drew the cable tight until it caught. Unable to move forward, the cable forced the speeding truck to flip end over end. From beneath the twisted metal of his totalled truck, the Joker crawled out, dirty but otherwise unscathed.

Batman revved up his bike, moving forward at high speed, prepared to chase down the Joker as he ran. But instead, the Joker rushed into the roadway, throwing his arms out, placing himself directly in the path of the oncoming Bat-Pod.

Batman was going too fast. There wasn't enough room on the Joker's left or right to swerve and miss him. He had two choices, hit him or crash.

Batman chose to crash. He locked his breaks and held on as the Bat-Pod slipped off the roadway, screeching out of control, finally slamming at full force into a large brick wall.

The Joker reached Batman first. He was barely conscious and having trouble pulling himself up. Joker took advantage of Batman's vulnerability and reached for his black cowl, ready to unmask the injured vigilante. An electric shock shot out from the mask and made him pull back his stinging hand.

Reaching into his purple coat pocket, Joker pulled out a switchblade.

The Joker leaned over Batman. If he couldn't take off the mask with his bare hands, he was going to cut it off. And maybe put a smile on Batman's face to match his own...

As the Joker crouched lower toward Batman, the armoured van skidded to a stop by the side of the road. The driver jumped out of the van, raised his weapon, and rushed over to arrest the Joker.

"Got you!" the driver announced, pulling off his SWAT helmet to reveal himself. It was Lieutenant Jim Gordon. The Joker dropped his knife, sorry that the evening's fun had ended.

The rear of the van opened and Harvey Dent came rushing forward. He couldn't stop grinning at the Lieutenant. "Back from the dead?"

Gordon shook the D.A.'s hand, "I couldn't chance my family's safety."

Dent nodded, nothing but respect in his eyes.

Gordon shoved the Joker into the back of a waiting squad car and drove off to MCU. Dent nabbed a ride home with Detective Wuertz, who was waiting for him by his squad car.

Batman managed to get himself on the Bat-Pod.

The police and Batman drove away in different directions.

It was over.

The Joker had finally been apprehended.

Chapter Sixteen

Barbara Gordon turned off the TV to answer the doorbell. She was stunned silent when she saw who was standing on her stoop. She fell against her husband, sobbing.

They held each other a short while before little James came out of his room, dressed in pyjamas, rubbing his eyes. "Who's there, Mama?" he asked.

She moved aside to let him see.

"Did Batman save you, Dad?" James Gordon Jr. asked, rushing into his father's open arms.

Gordon lifted his son tenderly, squeezing him tightly against his chest, and said, "Actually, this time I saved him."

The phone rang and Barbara went to answer it. "It's for you," she said, handing her husband the phone. "*Commissioner* Gordon."

Jim grinned as he reached for the phone.

Jim Gordon moved slowly through a room of detectives crowded in the observation room. They all wanted to talk to him, express how excited they were that he was actually alive, and congratulate him on his promotion.

It took a few more minutes than he'd wanted, but when he finally reached the holding cell, he knew exactly what he needed to do. There was a big problem and he was certain, beyond certain, that the Joker was involved.

He stormed into the room and, without preamble, said, "Harvey Dent never made it home."

"Of course not," the Joker replied calmly.

Gordon surveyed the man's pasty white make-up and snarled purple jacket. His detectives had told him they were having difficulty identifying who the Joker really was. But his identity wasn't Gordon's primary concern, finding Dent was.

"What have you done with him?"

The Joker laughed. "Me? I was right here. Who did you leave him with? Your people? Assuming of course they are your people, not Maroni's…" Gordon couldn't tell if the Joker continued to grin, or if it was just the way his mouth was deformed that made him look like he did.

"Where is he?" Gordon demanded to know.

Leaning back comfortably in the cold metal chair, the Joker looked at his wrist, as if he were checking a watch. "What time is it?" he asked.

"What difference does that make?" Gordon asked, losing patience.

"Depending on the time," the Joker said with a chuckle, "he might be in one spot. Or several."

Commissioner Gordon walked over to the Joker and undid his handcuffs. "If we're going to play games, I'm going to need a cup of coffee," the new Commissioner said.

The Joker knew the routine. The good cop leaves, and the bad cop comes in for a more intense questioning.

"The good cop, bad cop routine?" the Joker asked.

Gordon paused, one hand on the doorknob. "Not exactly," he replied before exiting the room.

FLICK! The overhead lights came on full bright. The Joker blinked against the glare.

WHAM! The Joker's face hit the table and the moment he

came back up for air - CRACK! CRACK! Two smacks on the head and then a dark form blocked the light. The Joker looked up to find Batman staring down at him.

"You wanted me? Here I am."

The Joker was bleeding, but didn't act as if he was in any pain. "I wanted to see what you'd do. And you didn't disappoint." He giggled at Batman. "You let five people die. Then you let Dent take your place. Even to a guy like me, that's cold…"

Batman hovered over the Joker. "Where's Dent?" His voice exploded in the small, closed room.

The Joker started laughing.

Batman asked another question: "Why do you want to kill me?"

Now the Joker was laughing so hard it sounded like crying. "Kill you? I don't want to kill you. What would I do without you? Go back to ripping off Mob dealers? No, you-" He pointed at Batman. "You. Complete. Me."

Batman shook his head. "You're garbage who kills for money."

The Joker replied, "We're exactly the same. And as soon as the chips are down, people will turn against you. To them, you are a freak like me. They just need you right now. But as soon as they don't, they'll cast you out like a leper."

"I'm not a monster," Batman countered. "I'm just ahead of the curve." With that, Batman grabbed the Joker and pulled him upright. "Where's Dent?" In one super swing, he tossed the Joker against the wall.

The Joker didn't even groan. Instead, he picked himself up, saying, "You live by society's rules and you think they'll save your soul."

"I only have one rule." Batman grabbed the Joker by his neck. "No one dies by my hand."

"Then that's the one you'll have to break to know the truth."

"And the truth is?" Batman was listening.

"The only sensible way to live in this world is without rules. Tonight you're going to break your one rule," the Joker told Batman.

Tightening his grip on the Joker's throat, Batman leaned in closer to his face. "I'm considering it."

The Joker choked out his next sentence. "There are just minutes left so you'll have to play my little game if you want to save…" He paused a beat. "…one of them."

Batman felt his blood boil. "Them?!" He opened his grip and let the Joker slam against the floor.

"For a while I thought you really were Dent, the way you threw yourself after her-" The Joker knew about Rachel. The Joker had Rachel!

In his anger, Batman ripped a bolted chair up off the floor. Batman jammed the chair under the doorknob, securing it shut. He didn't want the police stopping him from what he needed to do. In a lightening swift move, Batman grabbed the Joker and flung him, hard, against the two-way glass. The glass cracked, and the Joker was bleeding, but he still wasn't talking.

"WHERE ARE THEY?" Batman bellowed.

"Killing is making a choice," the Joker simply replied. "You will now choose one life over the other. Your friend the District Attorney. Or his blushing bride to be." The Joker grinned as he lay out the choices for Batman.

"You have nothing," the Joker said, laughing. "Nothing to threaten me with. But don't worry. I'm going to tell you where they are. Both of them. You'll have to choose."

Batman could only stare at the Joker, furious at this terrible game he was playing. Torn up inside that he was going to have to play along and pick one life over the other. Rachel or Harvey Dent. Who would he save?

"Dent is at 250 52nd Blvd. And Rachel is on Avenue X at Cicero." The Joker raised his eyebrows, challenging Batman to make his choice.

Batman gave the Joker one last swift kick in the side and hurried out into the night.

In another part of the building, one of the Joker's thugs was writhing on the floor of his jail cell. He was complaining to the guards that a severe pain was coming from something under his skin.

A guard checked him out and noticed that an odd rectangular shape was visible, just above his navel.

Meanwhile, the Joker was asking for a cell phone to make his one legal phone call. Reluctantly, a detective handed him a phone. With a hearty laugh, the Joker pressed send and…

The thug's belly began to glow blue. "Is that a phone?" the guard asked, bending in for a closer look at the thug's stomach.

BLAM! The phone inside the thug blew up, destroying the back wall of MCU and levelling that part of the building into a pile of rubble and debris.

Under the cover of the chaos he'd created, the Joker simply

walked out of his holding cell and entered the main part of the smouldering building. After a quick stop to make certain that the traitor to the mob, Chairman Lau of L.S.I. Holdings, was killed in the blast, the Joker freed himself from jail, whistling as he disappeared into the night.

Chapter Seventeen

In a basement apartment, in the dark, Rachel Dawes was all alone. She was tied to a chair, scared, but holding on to the hope that she would soon be rescued.

"Can anyone hear me?" she called out into the empty space.

"Rachel, is that you?" It was Harvey. Rachel struggled against the ropes that were holding her. She couldn't move. Looking around, squinting in the blackness, she spotted the source of Harvey's voice. A small speaker was on the ground, near her chair. Rachel discovered something else, too. Behind the speaker stood metal barrels, hooked to a car battery and a clock. The timer read five minutes.

Rachel started to cry.

Dent spoke softly, comforting her. "It's okay Rachel. Everything's going to be just fine."

Harvey Dent was also tied to a chair. In another basement. Across town from Rachel. He shoved his feet on the ground, hard and firm. He quickly discovered he could move his chair with the power of his legs. Slam. Slam. His chair turned slightly. Now he could see his surroundings better.

Metal barrels. Car battery. A timer that read: 3:15. And counting.

"Can you move your chair?" Harvey asked Rachel through the speaker.

tham's new District Attorney, Harvey Dent, is determined to stop the city's crime wave.

Alfred remains Bruce's most trusted friend and confidante.

Bruce Wayne must grapple with the complications of his double life as Batman.

Rachel Dawes finds herself drawn to both Bruce Wayne and her boss, Harvey Dent

Batman's upgraded suit is state-of-the-art.

The Batmobile's new parking spot is underground.

The Bat-Pod is Batman's lateset vehicle for chasing down criminals.

The Joker is the toughest enemy Batman has ever faced.

She couldn't. It was up to him to try to stop his timer, which now said: 2:47… 2:46…

Dent dragged his chair, inches at a time across the cold, cement floor. "Look for something to free yourself," he told Rachel as he struggled to reach the barrels and battery. He was close, so close, when his chair suddenly caught in a ridge in the floor and Harvey Dent toppled over, slamming into a barrel and spilling what he immediately recognized as diesel fuel onto the floor.

"Harvey? What's happening?" Rachel called out as he was turning his head to the side. Still stuck to the chair, Harvey was unable to move. The left side of his face was pressed into the floor. He couldn't talk because he didn't want to open his mouth and swallow any of the fuel which was seeping into his cheek, his eye and his skin.

"They said only one of us was going to make it. They'd let our friends choose." Rachel sighed audibly. Her resignation was obvious even over the speaker. "Harvey," she said at last, as the seconds clicked away, "I want you to know something."

Dent was choking on fuel, but he didn't care. He had to say something to the woman he loved. "They're coming for you, Rachel," he assured her. "It's okay. Everything's going to be just fine." The fuel felt hot as it seeped into his submerged eye.

Ten seconds remained.

"I don't want to live without you. Because I do have an answer and my answer is 'yes.'" Rachel agreed to marry Harvey Dent.

WHAM! The solid basement door smashed open. Batman had arrived. He rushed inside, seconds to spare, only to discover it was Dent he was about to rescue, not Rachel.

The Joker had lied. He'd told Batman that Dent was at 250 52nd Blvd. and that Rachel was on Avenue X at Cicero. It was actually the opposite. He should have known, but his emotions had gotten the better of him and he hadn't thought it through. He hadn't realized.

Now, Batman could only hope Commissioner Gordon had reached Rachel in time.

The counter hit five seconds. Batman grabbed Dent to drag him out.

"No! Not me!" Dent shrieked. "Why did you come for me?!"

Over the loud speaker, Harvey Dent could hear Rachel's last words before the explosion ripped through the warehouse.

Very calmly, she said, "Somewhere…."

Batman pulled Harvey Dent from the basement death trap.

The fuel puddle he'd been laying in had seeped into the left side of his face. It penetrated his eye socket, his hair, his cheek, and the left side of his mouth, so that it didn't matter how quickly Batman dragged him away, sparks from the flaming building set his face afire.

He woke up later, with bandages covering his face, all alone at Gotham General Hospital.

While Batman was rescuing Harvey Dent, over at 52nd Boulevard, Commissioner Gordon desperately wanted to save Rachel. He was running, axe held high. Gordon had to get into that basement. He simply *had* to.

Four…Three…Two…One.

Commissioner Gordon was too late.

Twin explosions rocked the city. Shards of glass, floating debris and ash enveloped the night, blacking out the moon. And in the remains of what once were two warehouses, playing cards floated to the ground. Hundreds of playing cards. All jokers.

And Rachel Dawes was dead.

In Bruce Wayne's penthouse, Alfred took out Rachel's letter to Bruce and read it for the hundredth time.

Dear Bruce, I need to explain…I need to be honest and clear. I am going to marry Harvey Dent. I love him and want to spend the rest of my life with him. When I told you that if Gotham no longer needed Batman we could be together, I meant it. But I'm not sure the day will come when you no longer need Batman. I hope it does, and if it does I will be there but as your <u>friend</u>. I'm so sorry to let you down. If you lose your faith in me, please keep your faith in <u>people.</u>

Love now and always,

Rachel.

Alfred set the letter on a silver tray along with a cup of tea for Bruce. Bruce was slumped in a chair, looking out the window at the lights of Gotham City.

To reach him, Alfred had to step over carelessly discarded pieces of Batman. The cowl and gauntlets lay strewn on the marble floor. Black boots and pieces of suit were tossed to the side, fallen where Bruce had unceremoniously dumped them.

When Alfred entered the room, Bruce looked up, a desperate expression on his face. "Did I bring this on us? I thought I would inspire good, not madness."

Alfred poured Bruce a cup of steaming tea and handed it to him. "You have inspired good. Things were always going to get worse before they got better." Bending down, Alfred retrieved the cowl from the floor, holding out the mask to Bruce as he spoke. "Gotham needs you."

"Gotham needs its hero," Bruce replied. "And I let the Joker send him to the hospital." Bruce couldn't shake off the images of Harvey Dent being taken away in an ambulance.

"Which is why for now, they'll have to do with you." Alfred handed the cowl to Bruce. Reluctantly, Bruce accepted the black mask, searching in its empty eyes for greater meaning. Without glancing up, he asked, "Alfred, that bandit, in the forest in Burma, did you catch him?"

Alfred nodded.

"How?"

Alfred shifted uneasily, distracting himself for a moment by collecting Bruce's tea cup. He sighed and replied with full honesty, "We burned the forest down."

And with that, Alfred took Rachel's letter off the tea tray and tucked it in his pocket. He'd made a decision. This was a letter Bruce Wayne would never see.

At Gotham General Hospital, Commissioner Gordon entered Harvey Dent's room. Gordon could only see the right half of Dent's face, but from this angle, he seemed to have come out of the explosion unscathed. Commissioner Gordon was baffled. He had heard that Dent had substantial injuries.

"I'm sorry about Rachel," Gordon said softly, then waited patiently for Dent to reply. But Dent said nothing. He just kept his face turned toward the small window in the hospital room. Gordon broke the silence. "The doctor says you are in agonizing pain but won't accept medication. That you're refusing skin grafts-"

Dent interrupted Gordon, not commenting on the medication, but asking a question instead. "Remember that name you all had for me when I was at Internal Affairs? What was it, Gordon?"

"Harvey, I can't-" Gordon protested. It wasn't a very nice name.

"SAY IT!" Dent shrieked, his voice echoing off the walls.

Commissioner Gordon looked away. He was embarrassed that his team had ever called Harvey Dent names behind his back. "Two Face," he said softly. "Harvey Two Face."

And with that, Dent turned in his hospital bed, showing Gordon the other side of his face. His left eye was grotesque, his cheek hallowed, his gruesome teeth were barely attached to the equally gruesome gums.

Gordon gasped, then immediately regretted it.

He could see Harvey's anger grow. The muscle in Dent's cheek twitched as he managed a small smile with the good side of his face.

"Why should I hide who I am?" Dent asked, his voice bitter and scathing.

Gordon took a deep breath and apologized from his heart. "I'm sorry, Harvey."

Harvey Dent was not accepting Gordon's apology. He never would. "No, you're not," he responded. "Not yet."

Bruce and Alfred were sitting together in the penthouse, when Mike Engel's voice attracted them to the television. Both men stared at the screen.

Engel was in the studio, addressing the camera directly.

"We have with us today a credible source. A lawyer for a prestigious consultancy. He says he waited as long as h e could for the Batman to do the right thing. But now he's taking matters into his own hands. We'll be live at five with the true identity of the Batman, stay with us."

The camera moved to a small man sitting at the table next to Engel. It was Reese, the man who'd tried to blackmail Lucius Fox with the drawings of the Batmobile that he'd discovered. Fox had told Bruce the story, but Fox had also assured Bruce that the man had been dissuaded. Apparently not.

On television, Reese appeared confident. After a short commercial break, Engle began taking viewer calls.

"Caller, you are on the air," Engel said, oozing with a reporter's charm.

"Harvey Dent didn't want us to give in to this maniac. You think you know better than him?" The caller was irate.

Engel responded, saying, "The guy's got a point. Dent didn't want Batman to give in. Is this the right thing to do?"

Reese pulled himself up, sitting straight. "If we could talk to Dent right now, he might feel differently."

Engel nodded. "And we wish him a speedy recovery. Let's take another call."

An old lady came on the line. "Mr. Reese," she asked. "What's more valuable? One life or a hundred?"

Reese didn't hesitate. "I guess it would depend on

the life."

The old lady continued her question. "Let's say it's your life. Is it worth the lives of several hundred others?"

"Of course not," Reese replied.

The caller's voice dropped. It wasn't an old lady at all. It was a man. "I'm glad you feel that way, because I've put a bomb in one of the city's hospitals. It's going off in sixty minutes unless someone kills you."

Bruce would have recognized that cackle anywhere. It was the Joker and he was playing his deadly games again.

"I had a vision," the Joker went on in his regular tone. "Of a world without Batman. I didn't like it at all. I don't want Mr. Reese spoiling everything, but why should I have all the fun? Let's give someone else a chance."

Reese was obviously growing nervous. He was sweaty and twitching.

"If Coleman Reese isn't dead in sixty minutes, then I blow up a hospital."

At that, the line went dead and the Joker's next game had begun.

Down at MCU, Commissioner Gordon flicked off the television.

"Call in every officer!" he shouted to anyone within hearing range. "The priority is Gotham General Hospital. Wheel everybody out of that place right now. My hunch is that's where the bomb is."

"Why Gotham General?" Detective Murphy asked.

Gordon took a deep breath. They were going to have to move at lightening speed. "Because that's where

Harvey Dent is."

Chapter Eighteen

The police rushed to the hospital where evacuations had begun. The patients, nurses, and doctors were all being loaded onto local school buses to be taken to safe spots throughout the city.

Gordon himself jumped into a police van and headed off in a different direction.

He pulled up in front of the television station and barrelled through the door, not stopping for security. Gordon was afraid that someone, probably someone with a family member in jeopardy at the hospital, would shoot Mr. Reese in order to save their ill relative from the Joker's sick plot.

Gordon arrived just in the nick of time. Upon entering the station, he immediately subdued an older man who had raised a gun, pointing it at Reese's head.

Moving swiftly, Gordon managed to knock the gun out of the man's hand and pull Reese into a back stairwell and down into the street.

"They're trying to kill me," Reese exclaimed, shaken from the attempt on his life.

Gordon stuffed Reese into the back of the van and then forced himself to smile. "Maybe Batman will save you," he said sarcastically. The van peeled out into traffic.

Bruce Wayne was rushing out of the penthouse, Alfred following closely behind, waiting for instructions.

"I need you plugged in," he told Alfred. "Check out Gordon's men and their families."

Alfred gave Bruce a questioning glance, "Looking for?"

"Hospital admissions," Bruce said, grabbing a set of car keys off a table near the door. He explained his suspicions that one of the detectives might want to take out Reese himself in order to protect a family member in the hospital.

Alfred agreed to start searching the hospital records immediately. "Will Batman be making an appearance at Gotham General?" he asked.

Bruce jingled the keys in his hand. "In the middle of the day? Not very subtle, Alfred."

Alfred watched Bruce as he stepped into the elevator and said with a sigh, "Ah yes, he's driving the virtually unnoticeable Lamborghini." He shook his head, thinking of the rare, high tech car that drew attention wherever it went. "That's much more subtle."

It was complete chaos. Bruce slowed the Lamborghini to a crawl in order to watch for a silent moment. Patients and staff were running around, pushing the infirm on gurneys and wheelchairs, IV bags swinging wildly. Cops and traffic wardens were feebly attempting to manage the evacuation.

He pulled over and parked near Gordon's white police van. Knowing that Reese was inside, Bruce felt sure that the van was a target for some nut who was out to do the Joker's bidding. There was someone out there who was planning to kill Coleman Reese.

Bruce kept one eye on the van while he continued to watch the patients as they were loaded on a number of different busses borrowed from the local schools. The minute one bus was full, it would speed away.

A TV van pulled up next to one of the buses, and Bruce saw reporter Mike Engel hop out with a camera man. The two men stepped onto one of the busses. Bruce figured they were going to interview the evacuees for a live broadcast.

His attention shifted away from the bus. There was an unmarked white truck barrelling at top speed toward Gordon's police van.

There wasn't time to consider what to do. Bruce had to act immediately. He revved the Lamborghini's engine and pulled out into the roadway. The truck was coming fast, but Bruce's million dollar souped-up car could move even faster. He slipped into the narrow space between the police van and oncoming truck.

WHAM! The truck hit the Lamborghini fully in the side, sending it reeling.

The police van was unscathed.

A swarm of police descended immediately and Gordon's men picked up the driver of the truck.

Commissioner Gordon jumped out of his van and hurried over to check out the driver of the Lamborghini.

There was a puzzled look on his face as he helped Bruce out of the completely totalled sports car. "You okay, Mr. Wayne?"

Bruce wavered, a little unsteady on his legs. It was one thing for Batman to take a hit in the armoured Batmobile. This was something entirely different. Bruce truly felt a bit woosy when he said, "I think so."

Gordon put an arm around Bruce to help him find his balance. "That was a brave thing you did," he threw a glance between the white truck and the police van.

Bruce wouldn't go there. His secret life had to remain secret. "Trying to catch the light?" Bruce asked as if he had simply been in the wrong place at the wrong time.

Gordon was baffled. "You weren't protecting the van?"

Bruce looked blank then, following Gordon's gaze, he looked at the police van as if seeing it for the first time. "Why? Who's in it?"

Coleman Reese stepped out of the van, dazed. He discovered Bruce looking at him and their eyes locked. Bruce knew his secret was now safe with Reese.

"You don't watch a whole lot of news, do you Mr. Wayne?" Gordon asked.

Bruce casually shrugged. "The news can get a little intense," he remarked with a grimace. Gordon backed away from Bruce, allowing him to stand fully on his own.

"Think I should go to the hospital?" Bruce asked, tilting his head to the nearby Gotham General.

Gordon smirked. "Not today, I wouldn't."

The hospital was deserted. And Reese was still alive. That meant playtime for the Joker had come. He laughed as he walked slowly through the empty halls pressing the large red button on his detonator. Blasts exploded behind him, one after another like the steady beats of a drum. It was wonderful. Hysterical. And the Joker enjoyed every minute of it as he strolled, grinning madly, out of the hospital and onto a waiting school bus.

After igniting one last enormous explosion, he gave a thumbs-up to the bus driver. The Joker had pulled off a prank once again, completely unnoticed. The bus merged into traffic and headed off to the next stop, where the Joker's full day of games and amusement was about to continue in grand style. He had plans and the destruction of Gotham General Hospital was only the beginning.

The explosion of the hospital could be heard for miles. Commissioner Gordon was still standing by his van when the hospital crumbled into a pile of rubble.

He had one thought and only one. "Did we get Dent out?" he asked a harried- looking officer, overwhelmed by the flow of evacuees he was directing across the street.

The cop looked up at his boss and replied simply, "I think so…" He scratched his head and then went back to helping patients move to safety.

When the Joker destroyed the hospital, Dent hadn't cared. He had been on his way out anyway. Refusing basic medical care like pain killers or reconstructive surgery, he spent his time concocting a plan to find those who had taken Rachel from him and to make them suffer.

During the chaos the Joker had caused at the hospital, Dent had walked out unnoticed and came straight to 250 52nd Street, the place he'd always consider Rachel's tomb.

A glitter in the burned-out wreckage caught his eye. Harvey Dent bent low and picked up his very own silver dollar coin. He'd given the coin with two heads to Rachel before the prison convoy had left the MCU. It had been shiny and pristine then.

Dent studied the coin in his hand. Now, it was charred. Blackened from the deadly explosion. On one side, the face had a huge scar across it. Dent flipped the coin over in his hand. Ironically, the other side looked as good as new. Clean and clear. In perfect condition.

As Dent rubbed his coin between his fingers, anger and frustration and sorrow consumed him until he could no longer think clearly. He *had* to know who it was that had picked up Rachel that fateful night and taken her to the warehouse on 52nd Street to die. As a D.A., he was an expert in questioning a witness and he knew exactly where to begin.

In a dusky tavern in Gotham City, the bartender was watching the nightly news.

A man in a back booth was watching, completely detached because it was not his job to clean up Gotham tonight. He had done all that he had to do and now he was taking a much needed break.

"Hello, Detective Wuertz," a shadow said to the man in the booth.

Wuertz was overcome with fear and dread. It was as if he was seeing a ghost. He could barely get his words out, he was so scared. "Dent, I thought you was…" he whispered his next word, "dead."

"Half," Dent replied, moving gradually out of the shadow and into the light.

The left side of his face was hideously burned. The flesh covering his check was totally gone, exposing the bone beneath. His hair was singed and black. What was left of his eye was precariously perched in its socket, barely holding on by charred muscle and sinew. And the left side of his mouth revealed nothing but blackened teeth and decaying gums.

Dent snagged Wuertz's drink off the table and took a sip. Wuertz could only stare as the muscles in Dent's face retracted with each swallow.

"Who picked up Rachel, Wuertz?" he asked. The muscles in his left cheek pulsated.

"It must have been Maroni's men-" Wuertz began, but Dent stopped him cold by slamming his glass back onto the table.

"You, of all people, are gonna protect the other traitor in Gordon's unit?" Since Wuertz had been the one to drive him from the gun battle on Lower 5th to the warehouse at Cicero, Dent knew he'd been one of the two traitors in Gordon's unit. But who was the other?

"I don't know," Wuertz insisted. "He'd never tell me." Wuertz was sweating profusely. "I swear to god, I didn't know what they were gonna do to you."

"Funny," Dent said as he pulled his scarred coin from his pocket. "I don't know what's going to happen to you either."

Both men watched as the coin flipped in the air, spinning a few times over and then landing on the table top.

Scarred side up.

Dent pulled out his gun….

Chapter Nineteen

Batman slipped quietly into the R and D Department at Wayne Enterprises. He'd been working on a major project and now it was to be revealed. He waited patiently, watching the many computer screens in front of him flicker in the dimly lit room. Each monitor displayed a small area of Gotham City, but when viewed together as a whole, the entirety of Gotham glowed in an extraordinary, large-scale map.

It was only a matter of minutes before his "break in" would be reported to the company's CEO and Lucius Fox would head down to R and D to investigate what was going on.

"Beautiful isn't it?" Batman asked Lucius the instant he stepped off the elevator.

It was unclear what Fox had expected when he'd come to look into the security breach, but this definitely was beyond his imagination.

"Beautiful," Fox echoed, then added with great concern, "and unethical and dangerous." He gave Batman a piercing glare. "You've turned every phone in the city into a microphone."

Leaning past his boss, Lucius pressed a button on a keypad. The babble of a million conversations suddenly filled the room.

"Not just a phone," Batman said over the noise, "but a high frequency generator/receiver, too."

Fox shook his head vehemently. His anger was palpable.

"Like the phone I gave you in Hong King. You took my sonar concept and applied it to everybody's phone in the city. With half the city feeding you sonar you can image all of Gotham." He flicked off the switch that controlled the sound. "This is wrong!" he exclaimed.

"I've got to find this man, Lucius," Batman explained.

Fox calmed a bit before responding, "But at what cost?"

Batman stood, pushing his empty chair toward Lucius. "The database is null-key encrypted. It can only be accessed by one person," he said.

Fox looked down at the chair and replied, "No one should have that kind of power."

Batman tugged his gauntlets into place and replied, "That's why I gave it to you. Only you can use it."

Lucius looked hard at Batman. "Spying on thirty million people wasn't in my job description."

In the centre of the room, above the monitors, a television screen glowed red, then blue, then popped to life with the image of the Joker. "What does it take to make you people want to join in the fun?" the Joker asked, his harlequin's grin striking horror in the hearts of Gotham's citizens. "You failed to kill the lawyer. I've got to get you off the bench and into the game. So here it is." His face moved closer to the camera lens, filling every inch of the television screen. "Come nightfall, this city is mine, and anyone left here plays by my rules. If you don't want to be in the game, get out now."

Batman could only imagine the traffic jams that were about to begin. There were very few ways out of Gotham City. There were the bridges, the tunnels, and- but Batman's train of thought was interrupted.

With a sinister laugh, the Joker added, "But the bridge and tunnel crowd are in for a surprise." And with that, his image faded to static.

Fox turned from the TV to look at Batman. Fox's calm demeanour was shaken.

"Trust me," Batman told him. His fingers flew over the console. "This is the audio sample that we just grabbed." Batman plugged in a USB cord. "The city is an open book." Lucius shook his head. He didn't want the power Batman was offering. He didn't want to spy on the entire city. "When you've finished, type your name in to switch it off."

Batman was on the move, ready to see what he could do to prevent more innocent lives from being lost this night.

"I'll help you this one time," Fox said as he sat in the chair Batman had given up. "But consider this my resignation."

Batman had nearly reached the elevator bank when Fox's words made him stop and turn. He knew from the expression on his CEO's face that Fox was serious.

"As long as this machine is at Wayne Enterprises, I won't be," Fox declared and, with that, began to scour the city, listening in on conversations, spying on everyone, with the hope that he would quickly determine the Joker's exact location.

Gothamites were pouring into the streets, anxious to leave the city, but getting out was complicated. Because of the Joker's threats, the bridges and tunnels were deserted while the bomb squad searched them inch by inch.

Mob Boss Sal Maroni was out of jail on bail and free as bird, while he awaited trial.

Without a concern in the world, he slipped into his limo, dressed fashionably for a night on the town.

He leaned back in his seat and spread out, getting comfortable. "Don't stop for lights, cops, nothing," he instructed his driver.

As the car drove off, Harvey Dent leaned forward into the light. Maroni gasped, but it was unclear if his rapid breathing was because Dent surprised him or because of Dent's deformed face. Dent demanded to know who took Rachel to the warehouse on 52nd. Maroni was the one who had bought the crooked cops the Joker used that night. They were Maroni's pawns. Wuertz and someone else. Dent needed a name.

"Take it up with the Joker," Maroni told Dent. "He killed your woman. Made you like this." He waved a gloved hand toward Dent's face.

"The Joker's just a mad dog. I want whoever let him off the leash," Dent pulled out a pistol and flashed the barrel at Maroni.

Maroni looked worried. He didn't want to die. "If I tell you, will you let me go?"

"It can't hurt your chances," Dent said with a non-committal shrug.

"It was Ramirez," Maroni squealed.

Dent took a silent minute to absorb his discovery, then he pulled out his silver coin. He cocked his pistol and flipped the coin.

"But you said..." Maroni began.

"I said it couldn't hurt your chances," Dent replied, catching the coin mid-air and looking at it. The smooth, clean side was up.

"Lucky guy," Dent said, and then he flipped the coin again. Maroni shook his head, confused, as Dent looked down at the coin in his hand. "But he's not," Dent said, faking his sorrow.

"Who?"

With the good side of his face, Dent smiled.

"Your driver," Dent replied as he pressed the barrel of the gun into the driver's back. Maroni screamed. Dent fired and then dove out of the limo, shooting off the door handles behind him as he rolled into the street so that Maroni was trapped. The limo swerved off a bridge, soaring out over a canal and finally crashing into a retaining wall.

Commissioner Gordon called the Mayor's office. He had news. Harvey Dent had not been found amongst the evacuees from the hospital. And worse than that, a bus filled with hospital staff and patients was also missing. Gordon was on his way to the docks to oversee the evacuation of Gotham citizens by ferry. The city was able to procure two ferries, and each one could carry about eight hundred people.

Gordon knew that only a small percentage of the city's population could be rescued this way, but there wasn't another choice. He told the Mayor that the prisoners associated with the mob that Dent had put away needed to be moved. The two men agreed; one ferry would be used for civilians. The second, for the prisoners.

Thirty thousand people arrived for eight hundred ferry seats. Full to capacity, the commander of the National Guard told both boats to head out. They were headed to the nearby coast and would get there as quickly as possible.

On the prisoner ferry, the first mate was getting a creepy feeling that something wasn't right. At first he thought it was just nerves. He was on a boat with nearly eight hundred prisoners and their armed guards. But that wasn't it. Something else was giving him goose bumps. He looked out at the water. It was so dark and foreboding. *Too dark*, he realized. He couldn't see the lights of the passenger ferry carrying Gotham's civilians.

The first mate immediately alerted his pilot. "They've lost their engines," he said calmly, though he wasn't feeling calm at all.

"Get on the radio and tell them we'll come back for them once we dump these scumbags," the pilot instructed.

The first mate was about to follow the order, with radio in hand, when suddenly the boat's control panel flickered and died.

"Get down to the engine room," the pilot instructed.

The first mate wasn't eager to go. He had to walk through the main room, past the prisoners and guards. The men jeered at him as he passed.

Down in the darkened engine room, the first mate discovered hundreds of barrels of diesel fuel strapped to a ticking bomb, and a small wrapped present, topped with a bow.

He grabbed the present and began his journey back, past the prisoners, to the bridge.

On the bridge of the civilian ferry, the pilot was holding a small, wrapped present, topped with a bow, identical to the one the first mate on the prisoner ferry found.

The pilot was talking into a crackling radio. "Same thing over here. Enough diesel to blow us sky high, and a present."

Speaking into the radio, the pilot from the second ferry asked, "Why would they give us the detonator to our own bomb?"

His question hung heavily in the air.

Above, a cell phone taped into the boat's ceiling wires rang and then answered itself. Nasty, evil laughter echoed through both ferries simultaneously.

"Tonight, you're all going to be part of a social experiment." The Joker stopped giggling and was all business. "Through the magic of diesel fuel and ammonium nitrate, I'm ready right now to blow you all sky high. Anyone attempts to get off their boat, you all die."

This was the Joker's grandest game of his whole criminal career.

"We're going to make things a little more interesting than that. Tonight, we're going to learn a little bit about ourselves." On both ferries, the radios died as the Joker cut off all communication to the outside world.

"There's no need for all of you to die. That would be a waste. So I've left you both a little present." The pilots of both boats looked down at the packages in their hands.

"Each of you has a remote to blow up the other ferry. At midnight, I blow you all up. If, however, one of you presses the button before then, I'll let that boat live. You choose. So who's it going to be – Harvey Dent's most wanted scumbag collection...or the sweet innocent civilians?" He paused a beat. "Oh, and you might want to decide quickly because the people on the other boat might not be so noble."

Once the rules of the game were delivered, Joker laughed one last laugh and clicked off the line.

The pilots both stared hard at their remotes, considering.

Barbara Gordon answered her telephone on the third ring. It was Anna Ramirez, one of her husband's detectives. Anna told Barbara that she needed to hurry and get out of the house. That it wasn't safe.

Anna gave her an address where Jim would meet her.

And Barbara believed everything she was told.

Outside MCU, Anna Ramirez hung up the telephone and handed it back to Harvey Dent. He was holding a gun to her head.

"She believe you?" Dent asked.

Holding back her emotions, Detective Ramirez didn't speak, choosing to nod instead.

"She trusts you," Dent pressed the gun into Ramirez's temple. "Just like Rachel."

Ramirez found her voice, "I didn't know-"

Dent finished her sentence for her, "-what they were gonna do? You're the second cop to say that to me. What, exactly, did you think they were going to do?"

Ramirez was not beyond begging for her life. "The mob got me early on. My mother's medical bills were too much for me to handle. I borrowed a little from them. Once they've got you, they keep you. I'm sorry-"

"Don't!" Dent didn't care about her sob story. He had his own troubles. It was time to discover the young cop's fate. He flipped his coin.

It landed on the good side.

"Live to fight another day, officer." Instead of shooting her, he cracked her on the head with his gun and left the MCU. He was off to his meeting with Barbara Gordon and her children.

On the prisoner boat, prisoners begin yelling and pushing. Concerned for the pilot's safely, the warden took the remote from the man and cocked his shotgun. As if on cue, the other guards levelled their weapons at the crowd.

In the main room of the commuter ferry, the National Guard Commander had taken over the remote. Several passengers looked as if they would kill to get it from him. Kill him, blow up the other boat, and save themselves. When one man took a step forward, the commander pulled out his weapon, saying, "Stay back!"

"We don't all have to die," a woman cried out from the rear of the crowd. She clearly thought they should blow up the prisoners.

"We're not talking about this." The commander held the remote firmly in his hand.

Another passenger reasoned, "They're talking over the same exact thing on the other boat."

Someone else suggested, "Let's put it to a vote."

Everyone agreed, so blank paper slips were handed out. The vote was "yes" to blow up the other boat, or "no" to hang tight and risk their own lives.

The civilian ferry pilot looked across the water at the other boat. He wished he knew what they were saying, and if they were voting. He pulled his eyes from the blackness and glanced at the clock. Ten to midnight. The National Guard Commander handed him his slip of paper. He was going to have to cast his vote.

Sitting atop an elevated roadway overlooking Gotham City, Batman searched the skyline for a sign of what the Joker was planning.

In the distance, he could see the ferries head out of port, and then lose power.

"Fox?" He needed immediate information. "There is something going on with the ferries."

Fox answered back right away. "His voice is on the ferry, but that's not the source." Batman could hear the clicking of typing as Lucius plucked away at the console keyboard. "I'm zeroing in."

Batman waited, his impatience growing. When he couldn't take it another second, he broke the silence. "Do you have a location on the Joker?"

"Head west." Lucius fired off directions as Batman fired up his engine.

Batman rang Commissioner Gordon. "I have the Joker's location," he said, revealing the address Lucius had given. Then Batman leaned close into the controls of the Bat-Pod, his cape folding down around him, and he peeled out, roaring into the night.

Batman met up with Commissioner Gordon on the rooftop

of a building facing a posh apartment tower known as the Prewitt Building.

Gordon's SWAT team leaders had already set up sniper and scope positions on the balustrade.

Gordon's radio blared with the bad news. "Down in the garage, we've found the missing school bus."

Gordon peered through binoculars at the place the SWAT team member indicated. He could see the bus sitting empty, deserted. "We have a hostage situation," he declared to his team members on the rooftop.

He scanned the building until he found what he was looking for. On the penthouse level, Gordon could see the Joker's men. They wore their clown masks and carried automatic weapons as they guarded a huddled group of patients, doctors, and nurses.

"We have clear shots on the five clowns. Snipers can take them out, smash the windows," a SWAT leader explained to Commissioner Gordon. "Then a team rappels in, and another team moves by the stairwells." He indicated on a blueprint map exactly where the stairwells were located. "There will be two or three casualties, max."

Commissioner Gordon barely hesitated. "Let's do it!"

Batman looked out over the side of the rooftop at the Prewitt Building. "It's not that simple. With the Joker, it never is." His mind was reeling with possibilities. He hadn't yet figured out what the Joker's game was in this instance. But now Batman clearly understood the man. Everything the Joker did was out of his twisted sense of fun. So what was he playing at this time? Batman didn't know, but he intended to find out.

"What's simple is that every second we don't take him, those people on the ferries get closer to blowing each other up," Gordon warned.

"That won't happen," Batman replied with complete certainty.

"Then he'll blow them both up!" Gordon was stressed. "There's no time – we have to go in now."

"There's *always* a catch with him." Batman didn't want Gordon to act impulsively. A lot of lives, both on the ferries and in the Prewitt building where they had located the Joker, were at risk.

"That's why we can't wait – we can't play his game." Gordon signalled his SWAT team to get ready.

Batman touched Gordon on the arm. "I need five minutes. Alone." He needed to get himself into the Joker's mind. To figure out-

"No." Gordon moved away from Batman's touch. "There's no time. We have clear shots now."

Gordon whipped out his gun. The SWAT team took aim.

"Dent disappeared from the hospital. He might have been on that bus! I think that Dent's in there with the hostages. We have to save Dent! *I* have to save Dent!" Gordon turned to his SWAT leader. "Get ready."

Undeterred by the SWAT team's weapons, Batman leapt in front of them, soaring off the rooftop, opening his cape as he spanned the gulf between the two buildings.

With an exasperated sigh and a streak of curse words, Gordon lowered his weapon. He turned to the SWAT leader and said, "Two minutes. Then you breach."

Chapter Twenty

SWOOSH! With winged grace, Batman softly landed against the glass exterior of the Prewitt building, two floors below where he knew the hostages were being held.

"Fox," he spoke directly, knowing his time was short. "I need a picture."

"You've got P.O.V. on alpha channel, omni on beta-" Fox reported as smoked-glass eyepieces slipped down over Batman's eye holes.

Through his sonar P.O.V., Batman watched the layers of the building slip away, levels of transparency pulsing rhythmically. Now Batman could see the people inside the building: the scared and shaken hostages, the armed guards, and most importantly, as he scanned though one last wall, he discovered the Joker, detonator in hand, staring out a huge glass window toward the two ferries in the distance.

Batman reached into his utility belt. He took out a canister and sprayed a thin sheet of plastic onto the glass before him. It hardened instantly. CRACK! Batman punched the window, which silently shattered as the pieces adhered to the spray-on laminate.

He slipped inside.

Using his eye piece, Batman planned his approach. His eyes glowed white as he looked around the corner. He could clearly see an armed clown leaning casually against the wall. Dogs barked in the next room, but Batman was focused on what was happening in this part of the building.

First things first.

Batman slammed the armed guard and the man dropped to the floor with a thud. Batman reached down to disarm him, but wait!

The weapon was duct taped to the man's hand. Batman wasn't quite sure what the Joker was playing at, but his instincts were burning. Something sinister was going on.

Batman ripped off the clown's mask. Staring back at him, eyes wide and full of fear, his mouth duct taped shut… it was the TV reporter…Mike Engel!

Batman recalled seeing Engel getting on a school bus with his cameraman back at Gotham General Hospital. Unwittingly, they'd climbed on the Joker's bus. And now Engel was in jeopardy with the rest of those who thought they were being driven to safety.

Using his sonar, Batman glanced into the next room. Four more clowns were standing by the window, weapons also duct taped to their hands.

Next he focused on the area where the hostages were crouched. The "patients" and "doctors" were all carrying weapons. It became crystal clear: The Joker had pulled a switch. The hostages were actually the Joker's men, pretending. The clowns, unloaded weapons taped to their hands, were patients and doctors forced into disguise as clowns.

Batman was horrified by the truth. He could hear the SWAT team rappelling down from the roof of the Prewitt Building and the clomp of boots climbing the stairs. The images flew through his mind. If the SWAT team attacked, they'd shoot the "clowns" and rescue the "hostages" and they'd have it all wrong! The innocent would die, the criminals would be saved.

"Don't move," Batman commanded Engel.

Terrified, Engel nodded.

Knowing Gordon, Batman was certain he'd given the SWAT leader on the neighbouring rooftop orders to shoot out the five clowns the man reported seeing though his rifle's scope.

Batman fired his grapple gun just in the nick of time. The rope wrapped itself around the legs of the clowns nearest to the window and toppled them to the floor in the same instant the glass of the window shattered under a hailstorm of bullets.

Diving and dodging the gunfire, Batman leaped up and wrestled two other clowns to the floor, saving their lives.

The SWAT team members were now on the move and Batman had no way to tell them that they had the situation backwards. All he could do now was try to save the innocent lives himself by fighting against Gotham's finest officers. It was deeply ironic, and that's exactly what the Joker wanted. Batman could imagine the man laughing himself silly in the room next door.

The SWAT team rappelled down the building. SLAM! They crashed in through the already broken window.

The "hostages" reeled from the blast. The SWAT team members swooped in, aiming their weapons at the clowns. It was pandemonium. The SWAT team members were throwing percussion grenades while Batman was fighting them off, taking them out with fists and Batarangs.

A SWAT team member raised his weapon at Batman. But behind him, Batman noticed a fake doctor pull out a real gun from his scrubs. Batman shook his head, overcome by the viciousness of the Joker's game. Now he must save a policeman who was trying to kill him from a disguised thug. And beyond the thug, he could see the rest of the SWAT team preparing to break in though the wall.

Batman vaulted over the SWAT team member, planting a two-footed kick into the thug's chest.

The rest of Gordon's SWAT team blasted through the wall. The team leader stepped through the hole first. Batman was on the move. His grapple fired out, lodging itself solidly in the man's Kevlar vest. The SWAT leader was yanked, screaming, away from the door. The rest of his team looked at each other, steeling themselves for a fight with Batman.

Racing in, the SWAT team discovered Engel, pale and shaking, sitting next to a pile of unconscious "hostages" and their own SWAT team leader, one end of a rappelling rope tied around his waist.

With uncertain expressions, they went after Batman, attacking with the full force of their training. Batman weaved, kicked, and downed SWAT members with one hand while clipping carabiners looped to the rappelling rope onto the webbing of their protective vests with his other hand.

When the men were connected like a link of chains, he stepped back. Batman raised the team leader high above his head and, ignoring the SWAT weapons trained at him, hurled the man out the nearest window.

The SWAT team were stunned stiff as they watched their leader fall out the window. The grappling rope paid out and, one by one, the six linked SWAT members were yanked out the window too.

They fell quickly until the line finally snapped tight and they hung off the side of the Prewitt building like a mountaineering team in crisis. Batman crouched in the broken window, working quickly to secure the line. His goal wasn't to kill the SWAT team members, just to get them out of the way so he could save the hostages. He'd let them hang around awhile until he'd finished his task.

The Joker was about to be brought to justice. There would be no more games.

Batman raced past a dazed Engel.

"Thanks," Engel said, sounding full of remorse for what he himself had done to disparage Batman's reputation.

Batman merely nodded and hurried into the next room, where the Joker was waiting.

Chapter Twenty-One

On the passenger ferry, the pilot tallied the votes. "One hundred, ninety-six votes against." He looked down at the other slips in his hand. "And three hundred, forty votes for."

Embarrassed by their own eagerness to blow up the prison ferry, the passengers avoided eye contact with each other.

Meanwhile on the other ferry, the corrections officers were cornered, struggling to keep hundreds of menacing prisoners at bay.

"Do *you* wanna die?" a prisoner asked his guard.

The warden and his men looked at each other helplessly.

Time was slipping away. A decision had to be made.

Batman didn't have to crash his way into the Joker's penthouse. The door was open for him, as if the Joker had been expecting him all the while.

"You came," the Joker said, welcoming his guest. "I'm touched."

There was no time for the Joker's nonsense. "Where's the detonator?" Batman demanded to know.

With a whistle and a casual wave of his hand, the Joker called in the Chechen's dogs. They were the Joker's dogs now.

The rabid dogs leapt on Batman, smashing him to the ground.

Batman wrestled with the rottweilers in a blinding mass of man versus fur and snarling teeth.

Batman fought valiantly, rolling over and over as he shook off each dog. Embroiled in the battle, Batman never saw Joker's attack coming. From the tip of his clown shoes, a switchblade popped out. The Joker moved into the swirling heap and just as Batman tossed off the last of the dogs, Joker found his target. He kicked his blade solidly into the vulnerable place between Batman's armour, straight into Batman's ribcage. "All the old familiar places," the Joker mocked, reminding Batman of their meeting in Wayne's penthouse when he'd first discovered that Batman had this weak spot.

Batman recoiled in pain. The Joker kicked him. Kneed him. Angry, evil energy filled the room and the Joker's attacks became more and more aggressive. He kicked and practically rolled Batman toward the glass window and a death drop to the street below.

The pilot of the passenger ferry stared solemnly at the remote in his hands. During the vote, the National Guard Commander had given him back the remote for safe keeping. But simply holding it would not keep any of them safe. The button needed to be pressed. Time was running out before the Joker killed them all.

"I voted for it," he told the waiting crowd. "Same as most of you. Doesn't sccm right that we should all die."

He had more to say, but someone from the back of the room shouted, "So do it!"

"I didn't say *I'd* do it," he explained. "Don't forget. We're still here. Which means they haven't killed us, yet, either."

He placed the remote on a bench at the front of the lounge and stepped away.

It was a silent dare. Who was willing to take the lives of eight hundred prisoners to save his or her own?

The other passengers and guards looked intently at the remote, but no one stepped forward.

A huge tattooed prisoner pushed his way to the front of the prison ferry. He didn't walk, rather he clomped with sure and determined steps toward the warden.

"You don't wanna die," the prisoner said to the warden, who was now holding the remote, beads of sweat dripping down from under his uniform cap. "But you don't know how to take a life. Give it to me." The tattooed prisoner held out his hand.

The warden's eyes darted from the remote to the clock and back again.

"These men will kill you and take it anyway," the tattooed prisoner told his guard. "Give it to me and I'll do what you should have done ten minutes ago."

At one minute to midnight, a businessman pressed his way through the crowd on the passenger ferry and picked up the remote.

"Fine. I'll do it," he declared. "No one wants to get their hands dirty. Those men on the other boat made their choices. They chose to murder and steal. It makes no sense for us to die, too." He glanced around at the other passengers, but no one would meet his eye. There was a palpable shame hanging over the crowd.

The business man's finger hovered over the red button. It moved lower and lower and the passengers braced themselves for the other ferry to explode.

He couldn't do it. With a resigned sigh, the man put the remote back on the bench, sat down next to it, head in hands, prepared to die.

The tattooed prisoner did exactly as he promised. He was going to do what the warden and the pilot and the first mate, what anyone should have done when they first found the detonator and heard the Joker's demands. He took the remote from the warden and promptly tossed it out the window. With a splash, it sunk to the bottom of the sea.

The clock struck midnight and Batman was in trouble. The Joker hurled his bruised and beaten body into the large viewing window in the penthouse of the Prewitt Building. CRACK! The glass gave way and with a crash the window's steel frame broke loose and dropped down toward Batman's neck.

Whipping his arms over his head, Batman was able to protect himself. The armour of his gauntlets was all the stood between him and sure death.

Batman grunted as he struggled to hold up the steel beam while shards of broken glass rained down all around him.

"If we don't stop fighting, we're going to miss the fireworks," the Joker remarked, casually stepping onto the steel beam that Batman was precariously supporting with his forearms.

"There won't *be* any fireworks," Batman groaned,

struggling to keep the beam from crushing his neck. He indicated the time. It was midnight. The ferries were both silent. "What were you hoping to prove? That deep down, we're all as ugly as you?"

The Joker looked at the clock on the penthouse wall. Disappointment showed on his face.

"You're alone," Batman told him, with gasping breaths.

The only smile now on the Joker's face was the one carved there. He bent low over Batman and showed him the dual remote. "Can't really rely on anyone these days." The Joker armed the remote control and readied it to destroy both ferries. "You have to do everything yourself." A smile returned to the Joker's face. "You know how I got these scars?"

Batman was still pinned under the steel beam. He looked up at the Joker.

"No," he said. He'd found a way out from under the beam. "But I know how you got this one." Batman's scalloped blades fired out of his gauntlet, nailing the Joker in the chest and arm. The clown staggered back, slipping off the steel beam and teetering on the edge of the window sill.

Free at last, Batman leapt forward, kicking the Joker over the ledge and grabbing the remote out of the funny man's hand.

Batman knew that the Joker wasn't afraid of death. He giggled as he fell, apparently enjoying the ride. But Batman could not break his one rule. The Joker would not die by his hand. He fired his grapple at the Joker's leg.

"Augh!" The Joker screamed as he snapped to a stop. Batman hauled him up, back into the shattered penthouse.

"Just couldn't let go of me, could you? Couldn't break up the team," the Joker mocked. Batman dumped the Joker back on the penthouse floor. The Joker stopped laughing just long enough to say, "You won't kill me out of some misplaced sense of self- righteousness and I won't kill you because you're too much fun. We're going to do this forever."

Batman shook his head. "You'll be in a padded cell, *forever*."

The Joker winked. "Maybe we can share it. They'll need to double up at the rate this city's inhabitants are losing their minds."

Batman knew the Joker was wrong. "*This city* just showed you it's full of people ready to believe in good." Batman tilted his head out toward he ferries, where the passengers had restrained themselves from blowing each other up.

The Joker looked at Batman. Where there should have been nothing but disappointment that he'd failed, there was still an odd twinkle in his eye.

"Just wait," the Joker bragged, "until they find out what I did with the best of them. Until they get a good look at the real Harvey Dent, and all the heroic things he's done." He too, tilted his head toward the ferries. "Those criminals will be straight back on the streets and Gotham will understand the true nature of heroism."

Batman hauled the Joker up, nose to nose.

"What did you do?!"

The Joker simply laughed, saying, "I took Gotham's white knight. And I brought him down to my level. It wasn't hard – madness is like gravity. All it needs is a little push."

The Joker began to laugh heartily now and Batman realized he'd been wrong. The game had not ended. There was more to come.

He turned the Joker over to the SWAT team and immediately called Commissioner Gordon to inform him that the Joker had another card up his sleeve.

Strange… Gordon didn't answer his phone. When Batman called, Gordon *always* answered his phone. Something was definitely wrong.

"Lucius," Batman called his CEO with great urgency, his adrenaline pumping at top speed. "It's not over. Find Harvey Dent!" He had a sneaking suspicion if he found Dent, he'd find Gordon, too.

Batman drew his cape around himself, preparing to forge on ahead on his difficult path, hoping that he didn't have to burn the city down to end the Joker's games.

Chapter Twenty-Two

Commissioner Gordon had received Dent's call while he was on the rooftop across from the Prewitt Building. Batman had entered the building, followed shortly by his SWAT team, but Gordon couldn't stay around to watch the Joker's capture. Gordon had thought that Dent was on the bus with the hostages the Joker had captured, but it turned out he wasn't there at all. He was at 52nd Street, in a burned-out warehouse, and he wanted Gordon to meet him there.

Commissioner Gordon felt the danger in his bones. His policeman's instincts told him something wasn't right. He removed his gun from its holster and slowly made his way into the shell of the building.

"Dent?" Gordon called out. There was no reply. Nothing but an eerie silence. He moved to the staircase and climbed to the second floor.

There was Barbara, huddled together with their two children. He hadn't expected to find them here and moved swiftly towards them, hoping to find out what was going on.

Barbara shook her head, as an impassioned warning.

WHAM! Dent cracked Gordon over the head with his gun. Gordon slumped to the floor, writhing in pain, while Dent took his weapon.

He didn't understand why the D.A. had turned against him and kidnapped his family.

"This is where they brought her, Gordon," Dent told the

commissioner. "After *your* people handed her over. This is where she suffered. This is where she died."

"I know. I was here. Trying to save her." Gordon wished he could tell Harvey how his own police force had had to restrain him. Even after the bomb had gone off, he'd struggled against his own men, trying to force his way into the building. It had been a devastating night for everyone who knew Rachel Dawes.

Dent turned to Gordon, with only his hideous, dark side showing. "But you didn't save her, did you?"

"I COULDN'T," Gordon shouted, as if loudness would somehow save him and his family. It was obvious what was happening. Dent was blaming Gordon for Rachel's death and was going to punish him by using his family as pawns.

"Yes, you could," Dent countered. "If you'd listened to me – if you'd stood up against corruption instead of doing your deal with the devil."

"I was trying to fight the mob." Gordon's eyes darted around the warehouse, searching for a way to move his family out of harm's way.

Dent moved closer to Barbara Gordon, gun raised against her.

"Harvey. Put down the gun." Gordon couldn't find another way out. He'd have to reason with the man. "You're not going to hurt my family."

"No, not all of them." Dent cocked his gun and pulled young James Gordon out from his mother's arms.

Tears streamed down Barbara's face. "No! Jim, stop him! Don't let him!"

Harvey Dent dragged the boy past his father, to the edge of

the hole in the burned-out floor. He tested the firmness of the floorboards with his foot. The floor wasn't steady. It could give way at any time.

"Let him go," Gordon said, maintaining an air of calm. "You're right, it's my fault Rachel died. Punish me instead."

When Dent made no sign of letting the boy loose, a deep voice called out to him from the shadows, issuing a stern warning. "You don't want to hurt the boy, Dent." Batman revealed himself.

"It's not about what I want. It's about what's fair," Dent told Batman. He held out his silver coin. "This boy has the same chance Rachel had. Fifty-fifty."

"Wait." Batman stepped in, closing the gap between Dent and himself. "Gordon's not the only one to blame. What about me? I'm the one who chose the other address. I had no right to choose."

Dent's grip on the boy loosened slightly as he considered Batman's words.

Sensing a slight change in Dent, Batman went on. "And what about you, Harvey? You made a choice. You knew the risks of pretending to be me. Shouldn't you deal with that before pointing a gun at an innocent?"

Dent was definitely listening. He stood quietly, deep in thought.

"Fair enough," he said when a decision had been made. "You first." He quickly flipped his coin, checked the result, and then shot Batman in the stomach. Batman collapsed onto the floor, holding his gut.

Then he turned his gun on Commissioner Gordon. "Your turn, Gordon." He tossed his coin up to determine the commissioner's fate.

While Dent's eyes followed the coin up, Batman peeled himself off the floor and hurled toward Dent and the boy. The three of them vanished into the hole in the floor. There was a terrible crash, followed by a deafening silence. The only sound in the warehouse was that of Dent's coin, spinning on the floor at the edge of the hole.

Horrified, Gordon rushed to the hole to discover the fate of his only son.

Dent was lying at the bottom of the hole, his neck broken.

But where were James and Batman?

The coin at the edge of the hole stopped spinning. It fell good side up.

Gordon's son suddenly swung into view, hanging from Batman, who was holding onto a joist with all his strength.

Gordon reached down and hauled up his son. As he did, the joist gave out and Batman fell, slamming through pipes and protruding wood, crashing to the floor below and landing next to Dent's broken body.

Handing James over to Barbara, Gordon ran down the stairs, rushing over to Batman. His son was close on his heels.

"Dad, is he okay?" James Gordon Jr. asked.

Gordon bent low over Batman. He nearly jumped out of his skin when Batman's hand reached up and grabbed his arm. Gordon helped Batman up.

"Thank you," Gordon said, helping steady the Caped Crusader.

"You don't have to thank me," Batman replied, his strength returning incrementally.

"Yes, I do," Gordon replied. Then Commissioner Gordon

sent his son to be with Barbara so that he could have a moment alone with Batman.

Standing together, Batman and Gordon looked down at Dent's body. "The Joker won," Gordon remarked. "He took the best of us and tore him down. Harvey's prosecution, everything he fought for, everything Rachel died for. Undone. The Joker has won and people will lose all hope." Gordon took a closer look at Dent's scarred face.

Batman reached down and turned Dent's face to show the pristine, good side. "No. They won't." He looked up at Gordon. "They can never know what he did."

Gordon couldn't believe what he was hearing. "People are dead because of Harvey Dent's choices. We can't sweep that under."

Batman sighed and stood tall next to Gordon. "No. But the Joker cannot win. Gotham needs its true hero."

Gordon understood. Batman was going to take the blame for the deaths Dent had caused. "You? You can't-"

Batman faced Gordon, quite serious. "Yes. I can." Batman recalled the words that Harvey Dent had once told him, not so long ago. "You either die a hero or live long enough to see yourself become the villain." He felt certain that what he was doing was the right thing. "I can do those things because I am not a hero, like Dent. I killed those people. That's what I can be."

Gordon was angry. Even in the darkness, it was obvious that his face had flushed bright red. "No, you can't! You're not!"

Batman handed Gordon his police radio. He was going to have to call in his troops. "I'm whatever Gotham needs me to be," Batman declared.

Gordon held the radio. "They'll hunt you."

Batman smiled. *"You'll* hunt me."

At Bruce Wayne's penthouse, Alfred tossed Rachel's final letter into the fire and watched as it smouldered, caught flame, and eventually turned to ash.

In the basement of Wayne Enterprises. Lucius Fox typed his name into the code screen of the sonar machine. He hit the "X." The machine flashed "self destruct warning," then died. Fox smiled to himself.

"Batman?!" James Gordon Jr. could only watch as the man who'd saved his life hurried out of the warehouse into the night. "Why's he running, Dad?!"

Gordon stared after Batman, listening to the roar of police sirens in the distance.

"Because we have to chase him," Gordon said, watching Batman leap from roof to roof, the police in hot pursuit. Later, he'd go to the roof of MCU and smash the Bat-Signal with an axe. Gordon knew that even if he used it to light the sky, Batman was not coming back.

"He didn't do anything wrong!" James Gordon Jr. exclaimed.

Dogs had joined the chase and Gordon could hear their barks splinter the quiet of the night.

"Why, Dad? Why?!"

"Because..." Gordon knew he needed to explain to his son what had happened. He wanted to get the words just right.

"He's the hero Gotham deserves, but not the one it needs right now. So we'll hunt him, because he can take it. Because he's not our hero. He's a silent guardian, a watchful protector... A dark knight."